THE

UPHILL CLIMB

B. M. Bower

The Uphill Climb

B. M. Bower

© 1st World Library – Literary Society, 2005
PO Box 2211
Fairfield, IA 52556
www.1stworldlibrary.org
First Edition

LCCN: 2006930763

Softcover ISBN: 1-4218-2173-7
Hardcover ISBN: 1-4218-2073-0
eBook ISBN: 1-4218-2273-3

Purchase *"The Uphill Climb"*
as a traditional bound book at:
www.1stWorldLibrary.org/purchase.asp?ISBN=1-4218-2173-7

1st World Library Literary Society is a nonprofit
organization dedicated to promoting literacy by:

- Creating a free internet library accessible from any
  computer worldwide.
- Hosting writing competitions and offering book
  publishing scholarships.

The Uphill Climb
contributed by Tim, Ed & Rodney
in support of
1st World Library Literary Society

CONTENTS

CHAPTER I

"MARRIED! AND I DON'T KNOW HER NAME!"

Ford lifted his arms above his head to yawn as does a man who has slept too heavily, found his biceps stiffened and sore, and massaged them gingerly with his finger-tips. His eyes took on the vacancy of memory straining at the leash of forgetfulness. He sighed largely, swung his head slowly from left to right in mute admission of failure to grasp what lay just behind his slumber, and thereby discovered other muscles that protested against sudden movement. He felt his neck with a careful, rubbing gesture. One hand strayed to his left cheekbone, hovered there tentatively, wandered to the bridge of his nose, and from there dropped inertly to the bed.

"Lordy me! I must have been drunk last night," he said aloud, mechanically taking the straight line of logic from effect to cause, as much experience had taught him to do.

"You was - and then some," replied an unemotional voice from somewhere behind him.

"Oh! That you, Sandy?" Ford lay quiet, trying to remember. His finger-tips explored the right side of his face; now and then he winced under their touch, light as it was.

"I must have carried an awful load," he decided, again unerringly taking the backward trail from effect to cause. Later, logic carried him farther. "Who'd I lick, Sandy?"

"Several." The unseen Sandy gave one the impression of a man smoking and speaking between puffs. "Can't say just who - you did start in on. You wound up on - the preacher."

"Preacher?" Ford's tone matched the flicker of interest in his eyes.

"Uhn-hunh."

Ford meditated a moment. "I don't recollect ever licking a preacher before," he observed curiously.

Life, stale and drab since his eyes opened, gathered to itself the pale glow of awakening interest. Ford rose painfully, inch by inch, until he was sitting upon the side of the bed, got from there to his feet, looked down and saw that he was clothed to his boots, and crossed slowly to where a cheap, flyspecked looking-glass hung awry upon the wall. His self-inspection was grave and minute. His eyes held the philosophic calm of accustomedness.

"Who put this head on me, Sandy?" he inquired apathetically. "The preacher?"

"I d' know. You had it when you come up outa the heap. You licked the preacher afterwards, I think."

Sandy was reading a ragged-backed novel while he smoked; his interest in Ford and Ford's battered countenance was plainly perfunctory.

Outside, the rain fell aslant in the wind and drummed dismally upon the little window beside Sandy. It beat upon the door and trickled underneath in a thin rivulet to a shallow puddle, formed where the floor was sunken. A dank warmth and the smell of wet wood heating to the blazing point pervaded the room and mingled with the coarse aroma of cheap, warmed-over coffee.

"Sandy!"

"Hunh?"

"Did anybody get married last night?" The leash of forgetfulness was snapping, strand by strand. Troubled remembrance peered out from behind the philosophic calm in Ford's eyes.

"Unh-hunh." Sandy turned a leaf and at the same time flicked the ashes from his cigarette with a mechanical finger movement. "You did." He looked briefly up from the page. "That's why you licked the preacher," he assisted, and went back to his reading.

A subdued rumble of mid-autumn thunder jarred sullenly overhead. Ford ceased caressing the purple half-moon which inclosed his left eye and began moodily straightening his tie.

"Now what'n hell did I do that for?" he inquired complainingly.

"Search *me*," mumbled Sandy over his book. He read half a page farther. "Do what for?" he asked, with belated attention.

Ford swore and went over and lifted the coffeepot from the stove, shook it, looked in, and made a grimace of disgust as the steam smote him in the face. "Paugh!" He set down the pot and turned upon Sandy.

"Get your nose out of that book a minute and talk!" he commanded in a tone beseeching for all its surly growl. "You say I got married. I kinda recollect something of the kind. What I want to know is who's the lady? And what did I do it for?" He sat down, leaned his bruised head upon his palms, and spat morosely into the stove-hearth. "Lordy me," he grumbled. "I don't know any lady well enough to marry her - and I sure can't think of any female lady that would marry me - not even by proxy!"

Sandy closed the book upon a forefinger and regarded Ford with that blend of pity, amusement, and tolerance which is so absolutely unbearable to one who has behaved foolishly and knows it. Ford would not have borne the look if he had seen it; but he was caressing a bruise on the point of his jaw and staring dejectedly into the meager blaze which rimmed the lower edge of the stove's front door, and so remained unconscious of his companion's impertinence.

"Who was the lady, Sandy?" he begged dispiritedly, after a silence.

"Search *me*" Sandy replied again succinctly. "Some stranger that blew in here with a license and the preacher and said you was her fee-ancy." (Sandy read

B. M. Bower

romances, mostly, and permitted his vocabulary to profit thereby.) "You never denied it, even when she said your name was a nomdy gair; and you let her marry you, all right."

"Are you sure of that?" Ford looked up from under lowering eyebrows.

"Unh-hunh - that's what you done, all right." Sandy's voice was dishearteningly positive.

"Lordy me!" gasped Ford under his breath.

There was a silence which slid Sandy's interest back into his book. He turned a leaf and was half-way down the page before he was interrupted by more questions.

"Say! Where's she at now?" Ford spoke with a certain furtive lowering of his voice.

"I d' know." Sandy read a line with greedy interest. "She took the 'leven-twenty," he added then. Another mental lapse. "You seen her to the train yourself."

"The hell I did!" Ford's good eye glared incredulity, but Sandy was again following hungrily the love-tangle of an unpronounceable count in the depths of the Black Forest, and he remained perfectly unconscious of the look and the mental distress which caused it. Ford went back to studying the meager blaze and trying to remember. He might be able to extract the whole truth from Sandy, but that would involve taking his novel away from him - by force, probably; and the loss of the book would be very likely to turn Sandy so sullen that he would refuse to answer, or to tell the truth, at any rate; and Ford's muscles were very, very sore. He did not feel equal to a scuffle with Sandy, just then. He repeated something which sounded like an impromptu litany and had to do with the ultimate disposal of his own soul.

"Hunh?" asked Sandy.

Whereupon Ford, being harassed mentally and in great physical discomfort as well, specifically disposed of Sandy's immortal soul also.

Sandy merely grinned at him. "You don't want to take it to heart like that," he remonstrated cheerfully.

Ford, by way of reply, painstakingly analyzed the chief deficiencies of Sandy's immediate relatives, and was beginning upon his grandparents when Sandy reached barren ground in the shape of three long paragraphs of snow, cold, and sunrise artistically blended with prismatic adjectives. He waded through the first paragraph and well into the second before he mired in a hopeless jumble of unfamiliar polysyllables. Sandy was not the skipping kind; he threw the book upon a bench and gave his attention wholly to his companion in time to save his great-grandfather from utter condemnation.

"What's eating you, Ford?" he began pacifically - for Sandy was a weakling. "You might be a lot worse off. You're married, all right enough, from all I c'n hear - but she's left town. It ain't as if you had to live with her."

Ford looked at him a minute and groaned dismally.

"Oh, I ain't meaning anything against the lady herself,"

Sandy hastened to assure him. "Far as I know, she's all right -"

"What I want to know," Ford broke in, impatient of condolence when he needed facts, "is, who *is* she? And what did I go and marry her for?"

"Well, you'll have to ask somebody that knows. I never seen her, myself, except when you was leadin' her down to the depot, and you and her talked it over private like - the way I heard it. I was gitting a hair-cut and shampoo at the time. First I heard, you was married. I should think you'd remember it yourself." Sandy looked at Ford curiously.

"I kinda remember standing up and holding hands with some woman and somebody saying: 'I now pronounce you man and wife,'" Ford confessed miserably, his face in his hands again. "I guess I must have done it, all right."

Sandy was kind enough when not otherwise engaged. He got up and put a basin of water on the stove to warm, that Ford might bathe his hurts, and he made him a very creditable drink with lemon and whisky and not too much water.

"The way I heard it," he explained further, "this lady come to town looking for Frank Ford Cameron, and seen you, and said you was him. So -"

"I ain't," Ford interrupted indignantly. "My name's Ford Campbell and I'll lick any darned son-of-a-gun -"

"Likely she made a mistake," Sandy soothed. "Frank Ford Cameron, she had you down for, and you went ahead and married her willing enough. Seems like there was some hurry-up reason that she explained to you private. She had the license all made out and brought a preacher down from Garbin. Bill Wright said he overheard you tellin' her you'd do anything to oblige a lady -"

"That's the worst of it; I'm always too damned polite when I'm drunk!" grumbled Ford.

Sandy, looking upon his bruised and distorted countenance and recalling, perhaps, the process by which Ford reached that lamentable condition, made a sound like a diplomatically disguised laugh. "Not always," he qualified mildly.

"Anyway," he went on, "you sure married her. That's straight goods. Bill Wright and Rock was the witnesses. And if you don't know why you done it -" Sandy waved his hands to indicate his inability to enlighten Ford. "Right afterwards you went out to the bar and had another drink - all this takin' place in the hotel dining-room, and Mother McGrew down with neuralagy and not bein' present - and one drink leads to another, you know. I come in then, and the bunch was drinkin' luck to you fast as Sam could push the bottles along. Then you went back to the lady - and if you don't know what took place you can search me - and pretty soon Bill said you'd took her and her grip to the depot. Anyway, when you come back, you wasn't troubled with no attack of politeness!

"You went in the air with Bill, first," continued Sandy, testing with his finger the temperature of the water in the basin, "and bawled him

B. M. Bower

out something fierce for standing by and seeing you make a break like that without doing something. You licked him - and then Rock bought in because some of your remarks kinda included him too. I d' know," said Sandy, scratching his unshaven jaw reflectively, "just how the fight did go between you 'n' Rock. You was both using the whole room, I know. Near as I could make out, you - or maybe it was Rock - tromped on Big Jim's bunion. This cold spell's hard on bunions - and Big Jim went after you both with blood in his eye.

"After that" - Sandy spread his arms largely - "it was go-as-you-please. Sam and me was the only ones that kept out, near as I can recollect, and when it thinned up a bit, you had Aleck down and was pounding the liver outa him, and Big Jim was whanging away at you, and Rock was clawin' Jim in the back of the neck, and you was all kickin' like bay steers in brandin' time. I reached in under the pile and dragged you out by one leg and left the rest of 'em fighting. They never seemed to miss you none." He grinned. "Jim commenced to bump Aleck's head up and down on the floor instead of you - and I knew he didn't have nothing against Aleck."

"Bill -"

"Bill, he'd quit right in the start." Sandy's grin became a laugh. "Seems like pore old Bill always gits in bad when you commence on your third pint. You wasn't through, though, seems like. You was going to start in at the beginning and en-core the whole performance, and you started out after Bill. Bill, he was lookin' for a hole big enough to crawl into by that time. But you run into the preacher. And you licked him to a fare-you-well and had him crying real tears before I or anybody else could stop you."

"What'd I lick him for?" Ford inquired in a tone of deep discouragement.

Sandy's indeterminate, blue-gray eyes rounded with puzzlement.

"Search me," he repeated automatically. But later he inadvertently shed enlightenment. He laughed, bending double, and slapping his thigh at the irresistible urge of a mental picture.

"Thought I'd die," he gasped. "Me and Sam was watching from the door. You had the preacher by the collar, shakin' him, and once in awhile liftin' him clean off the ground on the toe of your boot; and you kept saying: 'A sober man, and a preacher - and you'd marry that girl to a fellow like me!' And then biff! And he'd let out a squawk. 'A drinkin', fightin', gamblin' son-of-a-gun like me, you swine!' you'd tell him. And when we finally pulled you loose, he picked up his hat and made a run for it."

Ford meditated gloomily. "I'll lick him again, and lick him when I'm sober, by thunder!" he promised grimly. "Who was he, do you know?"

"No, I don't. Little, dried-up geezer with a nose like a kit-fox's and a whine to his voice. He won't come around here no more."

The door opened gustily and a big fellow with a skinned nose and a whimsical pair of eyes looked in, hesitated while he stared hard at Ford, and then entered and shut the door by the simple method of throwing his shoulders back against it.

"Hello, old sport - how you comin'?" he cried cheerfully. "Kinda wet for makin' calls, but when a man's loaded down with a guilty conscience -" He sighed somewhat ostentatiously and pulled forward a chair rejuvenated with baling-wire braces between the legs, and a cowhide seat. "What's that cookin' - coffee, or sheep-dip?" he inquired facetiously of Sandy, though his eyes dwelt solicitously upon Ford's bowed head. He leaned forward and slapped Ford in friendly fashion upon the shoulder.

"Buck up - 'the worst is yet to come,'" he shouted, and laughed with an exaggeration of cheerfulness. "You can't ever tell when death or matrimony's goin' to get a man. By hokey, seems like there's no dodgin' either one."

Ford lifted a bloodshot eye to the other. "And I always counted you for a friend, Bill," he reproached heavily. "Sandy says I licked you good and plenty. Well, looks to me like you had it coming, all right."

"Well - I got it, didn't I?" snorted Bill, his hand lifting involuntarily to his nose. "And I ain't bellering, am I?" His mouth took an abused, downward droop. "I ain't holdin' any grudge, am I? Why, Sandy here can tell you that I held one side of you up whilst he was leadin' the other side of you home! And I am sorry I stood there and seen you get married off and never lifted a finger; I'm darned sorry. I shoulda hollered misdeal, all right. I know it now." He pulled remorsefully at his wet mustache, which very much resembled a worn-out sharing brush.

Ford straightened up, dropped a hand upon his thigh, and thereby discovered another sore spot, which he caressed gently with his palm.

"Say, Bill, you were there, and you saw her. On the square now - what's she like? And what made me marry her?"

Bill pulled so hard upon his mustache that his teeth showed; his breath became unpleasantly audible with the stress of emotion. "So help me, I can't tell you what she's like, Ford," he confessed. "I don't remember nothing about her looks, except she looked good to me, and I never seen her before, and her hair wasn't red - I always remember red hair when I see it, drunk or sober. You see," he added as an extenuation, "I was pretty well jagged myself. I musta been. I recollect I was real put out because my name wasn't Frank Ford - By hokey!" He laid an impressive forefinger upon Ford's knee and tapped several times. "I never knew your name was rightly Frank Ford Cameron. I always -"

"It ain't." Ford winced and drew away from the tapping process, as if his knee also was sensitive that morning.

"You told her it was. I mind that perfectly, because I was so su'prised I swore right out loud and was so damned ashamed I couldn't apologize. And say! She musta been a real lady or I wouldn't uh felt that way about it!" Bill glanced triumphantly from one to the other. "Take it from me, you married a lady, Ford. Drunk or sober, I always make it a point to speak proper before the ladies - t'other kind don't count - and when I make a break, you betcher life I remember it. She's a real lady - I'd swear to that on a stack uh bibles ten feet high!" He settled back and unbuttoned his steaming coat with the air of a man who has established beyond question the vital point of an argument.

"Did I tell her so myself, or did I just let it go that way?" Ford, as his brain cleared, stuck close to his groping for the essential facts.

"Well, now - I ain't dead sure as to that. Maybe Rock'll remember. Kinda seems to me now, that she asked you if you was really Frank Ford Cameron, and you said: 'I sure am,' or something like that. The preacher'd know, maybe. He musta been the only sober one in the bunch - except the girl. But you done chased him off, so -"

"Sandy, I wish you'd go hunt Rock up and tell him I want to see him." Ford spoke with more of his natural spirit than he had shown since waking.

"Rock's gone on out to Riley's camp," volunteered Bill. "Left this morning, before the rain started in."

"What was her name - do you know?" Ford went back to the mystery.

"Ida - or was it Jenny? Some darned name - I heard it, when the preacher was marrying you." Bill was floundering hopelessly in mental fog, but he persisted. "And I seen it wrote in the paper I signed my name to. I mind she rolled up the paper afterwards and put it - well, I dunno where, but she took it away with her, and says to you: 'That's safe, now' - or 'You're safe,' or 'I'm safe,' - anyway, some darned thing was safe. And I was goin' to kiss the bride - mebbe I did kiss her - only I'd likely remember it if I had, drunk or sober! And - oh, now I got it!" Bill's voice was full of elation. "You was goin' to kiss the bride - that was it, it was you goin' to kiss her, and she slap - no, by hokey, she didn't slap you, she just - or was it Rock, now?" Doubt filled his eyes distressfully. "Darn my everlastin' hide," he finished lamely, "there was some kissin' somew'ere in the deal, and I mind her cryin' afterwards, but whether it was about that, or - Say, Sandy, what was it Ford was lickin' the preacher for? Wasn't it for kissin' the bride?"

"It was for marrying him to her," Sandy informed him sententiously.

Ford got up and went to the little window and looked out. Presently he came back to the stove and stood staring disgustedly down upon the effusively friendly Bill, leering up at him pacifically.

"If I didn't feel so rotten," he said glumly, "I'd give you another licking right now, Bill - you boozing old devil. I'd like to lick every darned galoot that stood back and let me in for this. You'd ought to have stopped me. You'd oughta pounded the face off me before you let me do such a fool thing. That," he said bitterly, "shows how much a man can bank on his friends!"

"It shows," snorted Bill indignantly, "how much he can bank on himself!"

"On whisky, to let him in for all kinds uh trouble," revised Sandy virtuously. Sandy had a stomach which invariably rebelled at the second glass and therefore, remaining always sober perforce, he took to himself great credit for his morality.

"Married! - and I don't so much as know her name!" gritted Ford, and went over and laid himself down upon the bed, and sulked for the rest of that day of rain and gloom.

CHAPTER II

WANTED: INFORMATION

Sulking never yet solved a mystery nor will it accomplish much toward bettering an unpleasant situation. After a day of unmitigated gloom and a night of uneasy dreams, Ford awoke to a white, shifting world of the season's first blizzard, and to something like his normal outlook upon life.

That outlook had ever been cheerful, with the cheerfulness which comes of taking life in twenty-four-hour doses only, and of looking not too far ahead and backward not at all. Plenty of persons live after that fashion and thereby attain middle life with smooth foreheads and cheeks unlined by thought; and Ford was therefore not much different from his fellows. Never before had he found himself with anything worse than bodily bruises to sour life for him after a tumultuous night or two in town, and the sensation of a discomfort which had not sprung from some well-defined physical sense was therefore sufficiently novel to claim all his attention.

It was not the first time he had fought and forgotten it afterwards. Nor was it a new experience for him to seek information from his friends after a night full of incident. Sandy he had always found tolerably reliable,

B. M. Bower

because Sandy, being of that inquisitive nature so common to small persons, made it a point to see everything there was to be seen; and his peculiar digestive organs might be counted upon to keep him sober. It was a real grievance to Ford that Sandy should have chosen the hour he did for indulging in such trivialities as hair-cuts and shampoos, while events of real importance were permitted to transpire unseen and unrecorded. Ford, when the grievance thrust itself keenly upon him, roused the recreant Sandy by pitilessly thrusting an elbow against his diaphragm.

Sandy grunted at the impact and sat bolt upright in bed before he was fairly awake. He glanced reproachfully down at Ford, who stared back at him from a badly crumpled pillow.

"Get up," growled Ford, "and start a fire going, darn you. You kept me awake half the night, snoring. I want a beefsteak with mushrooms, devilled kidneys, waffles with honey, and four banana fritters for breakfast. I'll take it in bed; and while I'm waiting, you can bring me the morning paper and a package of Egyptian Houris."

Sandy grunted again, slid reluctantly out into the bitterly cold room, and crept shivering into his clothes. He never quite understood Ford's sense of humor, at such times, but he had learned that it is more comfortable to crawl out of bed than to be kicked out, and that vituperation is a mere waste of time when matched against sheer heartlessness and a superior muscular development.

"Y' ought to make your wife build the fires," he taunted, when he was clothed and at a safe distance from the bed. He ducked instinctively afterwards, but Ford was merely placing a match by itself on the bench close by.

"That's one," Ford remarked calmly. "I'm going to thrash every misguided humorist who mentions that subject to me in anything but a helpful spirit of pure friendship. I'm going to give him a separate licking for every alleged joke. I'll want two steaks, Sandy. I'll likely have to give you about seven distinct wallopings. Hand me some more matches to keep tally with. I don't want to cheat you out of your just dues."

Sandy eyed him doubtfully while he scraped the ashes from the grate.

"You may want a dozen steaks, but that ain't saying you're going to git 'em," he retorted, with a feeble show of aggression. "And 's far as licking me goes -" He stopped to blow warmth upon his fingers, which were numbed with their grasp of the poker. "As for licking me, I guess you'll have to do that on the strength uh bacon and sour-dough biscuits; if you do it at all, which I claim the privilege uh doubting a whole lot."

Ford laughed a little at the covert challenge, made ridiculous by Sandy's diminutive stature, pulled the blankets up to his eyes, and dozed off luxuriously; and although it is extremely tiresome to be told in detail just what a man dreams upon certain occasions, he did dream, and it was something about being married. At any rate, when the sizzling of bacon frying invaded even his slumber and woke him, he felt a distinct pang of disappointment that it was Sandy's carroty head bent over the frying-pan, instead of a wife with blond hair

B. M. Bower

which waved becomingly upon her temples.

"Wonder what color her hair is, anyway," he observed inadvertently, before he was wide enough awake to put the seal of silence on his musings.

"Hunh?"

"I asked when those banana fritters are coming up," lied Ford, getting out of bed and yawning so that his swollen jaw hurt him, and relapsed into his usual taciturnity, which was his wall of defense against Sandy's inquisitiveness.

He ate his breakfast almost in silence, astonishing Sandy somewhat by not complaining of the excess of soda in the biscuits. Ford was inclined toward fastidiousness when he was sober - a trait which caused men to suspect him of descending from an upper stratum of society; though just when, or just where, or how great that descent had been, they had no means of finding out. Ford, so far as his speech upon the subject was concerned, had no existence previous to his appearance in Montana, five or six years before; but he bore certain earmarks of a higher civilization which, in Sandy's mind, rather concentrated upon a pronounced distaste for soda-yellowed bread, warmed-over coffee, and scorched bacon. That he swallowed all these things and seemed not to notice them, struck Sandy as being almost as remarkable as his matrimonial adventure.

When he had eaten, Ford buttoned himself into his overcoat, pulled his moleskin cap well down, and went out into the storm without a word to Sandy, which was also unusual; it was Ford's custom to wash the dishes, because he objected to Sandy's economy of clean, hot water. Sandy flattened his nose against the window, saw that Ford, leaning well forward against the drive of the wind, was battling his way toward the hotel, and guessed shrewdly that he would see him no more that day.

"He better keep sober till his knuckles git well, anyway," he mumbled disapprovingly. "If he goes to fighting, the shape he's in now -"

Ford had no intention of fighting. He went straight up to the bar, it is true, but that was because he saw that Sam was at that moment unoccupied, save with a large lump of gum. Being at the bar, he drank a glass of whisky; not of deliberate intent, but merely from force of habit. Once down, however, the familiar glow of it through his being was exceedingly grateful, and he took another for good measure.

"H'lo, Ford," Sam bethought him to say, after he had gravely taken mental note of each separate scar of battle, and had shifted his cud to the other side of his mouth, and had squeezed it meditatively between his teeth. "Feel as rocky as you look?"

"Possibly." Ford's eyes forbade further personalities. "I'm out after information, Sam, and if you've got any you aren't using, I'd advise you to pass it over; I can use a lot, this morning. Were you sober, night before last?"

Sam chewed solemnly while he considered. "Tolerable sober, yes," he decided at last. "Sober enough to tend to business; why?"

With his empty glass Ford wrote invisible scrolls upon the bar. "I - did you happen to see - my - the lady I married?" He had been embarrassed at first, but when he finished he was glaring a challenge which shifted the disquiet to Sam's manner.

"No. I was tendin' bar all evenin' - and she didn't come in here."

Ford glanced behind him at the sound of the door opening, saw that it was only Bill, and leaned over the bar for greater secrecy, lowering his voice as well.

"Did you happen to hear who she was?"

Sam stared and shook his head.

"Don't you know anything about her at all - where she came from - and why, and where she went?"

Sam backed involuntarily. Ford's tone made it a crime either to know these things or to be guilty of ignorance; which, Sam could not determine. Sam was of the sleek, oily-haired type of young men, with pimples and pale eyes and a predilection for gum and gossip. He was afraid of Ford and he showed it.

"That's just what (no offense, Ford - I ain't responsible) that's what everybody's wondering. Nobody seems to know. They kinda hoped you'd explain -"

"Sure!" Ford's tone was growing extremely ominous. "I'll explain a lot of things - if I hear any gabbling going on about my affairs." He was seized then with an uncomfortable feeling that the words were mere puerile blustering and turned away from the bar in disgust.

In disgust he pulled open the door, flinched before the blast of wind and snow which smote him full in the face and blinded him, and went out again into the storm. The hotel porch was a bleak place, with snow six inches deep and icy boards upon which a man might easily slip and break a bone or two, and with a whine overhead as the wind sucked under the roof. Ford stood there so long that his feet began to tingle. He was not thinking; he was merely feeling the feeble struggles of a newborn desire to be something and do something worth while - a desire which manifested itself chiefly in bitterness against himself as he was, and in a mental nausea against the life he had been content to live.

The mystery of his marriage was growing from a mere untoward incident of a night's carouse into a baffling thing which hung over him like an impending doom. He was not the sort of man who marries easily. It seemed incredible that he could really have done it; more incredible that he could have done it and then have wiped the slate of his memory clean; with the crowning impossibility that a strange young woman could come into town, marry him, and afterward depart and no man know who she was, whence she had come, or where she had gone. Ford stepped suddenly off the porch and bored his way through the blizzard toward the depot. The station agent would be able to answer the last question, at any rate.

The agent, however, proved disappointingly ignorant of the matter. He reminded Ford that there had not been time to buy a ticket, and that the girl had been compelled to run down the platform to reach the train before it started, and that the wheels began to turn before she was up the steps of the day coach.

B. M. Bower

"And don't you remember turning around and saying to me: 'I'm a poor married man, but you can't notice the scar,' or something like that?" The agent was plainly interested and desirous of rendering any assistance possible, and also rather diffident about discussing so delicate a matter with a man like Ford.

Ford drummed his fingers impatiently upon the shelf outside the ticket window. "I don't remember a darned thing about it," he confessed glumly. "I can't say I enjoy running all around town trying to find out who it was I married, and why I married her, and where she went afterwards, but that's just the kinda fix I'm in, Lew. I don't suppose she came here and did it just for fun - and I can't figure out any other reason, unless she was plumb loco. From all I can gather, she was a nice girl, and it seems she thought I was Frank Ford Cameron - which I am not!" He laughed, as a man will laugh sometimes when he is neither pleased nor amused.

"I might ask McCreery - he's conductor on Fourteen. He might remember where she wanted to go," the agent suggested hesitatingly. "And say! What's the matter with going up to Garbin and looking up the record? She had to get the license there, and they'd have her name, age, place of residence, and - and whether she's white or black." The agent smiled uncertainly over his feeble attempt at a joke. "I got a license for a friend once," he explained hastily, when he saw that Ford's face did not relax a muscle. "There's a train up in forty minutes -"

"Sure, I'll do that." Ford brightened. "That must be what I've been trying to think of and couldn't. I knew there was some way of finding out. Throw me a round-trip ticket, Lew. Lordy me! I can't afford to let a real, live wife slip the halter like this and leave me stranded and not knowing a thing about her. How much is it?"

The agent slid a dark red card into the mouth of his office stamp, jerked down the lever, and swung his head quickly toward the sounder chattering hysterically behind him. His jaw slackened as he listened, and he turned his eyes vacantly upon Ford for a moment before he looked back at the instrument.

"Well, what do you know about that?" he queried, under his breath, released the ticket from the grip of the stamp, and flipped it into the drawer beneath the shelf as if it were so much waste paper.

"That's my ticket," Ford reminded him levelly.

"You don't want it now, do you?" The agent grinned at him. "Oh, I forgot you couldn't read that." He tilted his head back toward the instrument. "A wire just went through - the court-house at Garbin caught fire in the basement - something about the furnace, they think - and she's going up in smoke. Hydrants are froze up so they can't get water on it. That fixes your looking up the record, Ford."

Ford stared hard at him. "Well, I might hunt up the preacher and ask him," he said, his tone dropping again to dull discouragement.

The agent chuckled. "From all I hear," he observed rashly, "you've made that same preacher mighty hard to catch!"

Ford drummed upon the shelf and scowled at the smoke-blackened window, beyond which the snow was sweeping aslant. Upon his own side of the ticket window, the agent pared his nails with his pocket-knife and watched him furtively.

"Oh, hell! What do I care, anyway?" Revulsion seized Ford harshly. "I guess I can stand it if she can. She came here and married me - it isn't my funeral any more than it is hers. If she wants to be so darned mysterious about it, she can go plumb - to - New York!" There were a few decent traits in Ford Campbell; one was his respect for women, a respect which would not permit him to swear about this wife of his, however exasperating her behavior.

"That's the sensible way to look at it, of course," assented the agent, who made it a point to agree always with a man of Ford's size and caliber, on the theory that amiability means popularity, and that placation is better than plasters. "You sure ought to let her do the hunting - and the worrying, too. You aren't to blame if she married you unawares. She did it all on her own hook - and she must have known what she was up against."

"No, she didn't," flared Ford unexpectedly. "She made a mistake, and I wanted to point it out to her and help her out of it if I could. She took me for some one else, and I was just drunk enough to think it was a joke, I suppose, and let it go that way. I don't believe she found out she tied up to the wrong man. It's entirely my fault, for being drunk."

"Well, putting it that way, you're right about it," agreed the adaptable Lew. "Of course, if you hadn't been -"

"If whisky's going to let a fellow in for things like this, it's time to cut it out altogether." Ford was looking at the agent attentively.

"That's right," assented the other unsuspectingly. "Whisky is sure giving you the worst of it all around. You ought to climb on the water-wagon, Ford, and that's a fact. Whisky's the worst enemy you've got."

"Sure. And I'm going to punish all of it I can get my hands on!" He turned toward the door. "And when I'm good and full of it," he added as an afterthought, "I'm liable to come over here and lick you, Lew, just for being such an agreeable cuss. You better leave your mother's address handy." He laughed a little to himself as he pulled the door shut behind him. "I bet he'll keep the frost thawed off the window to-day, just to see who comes up the platform," he chuckled.

He would have been more amused if he had seen how the agent ducked anxiously forward to peer through the ticket window whenever the door of the waiting room opened, and how he started whenever the snow outside creaked under the tread of a heavy step; and he would have been convulsed with mirth if he had caught sight of the formidable billet of wood which Lew kept beside his chair all that day, and had guessed its purpose, and that it was a mute witness to the reputation which one Ford Campbell bore among his fellows. Lew was too wise to consider for a moment the revolver meant to protect the contents of the safe. Even the unintelligent know better than to throw a lighted match into a keg of gunpowder.

Ford leaned backward against the push of the storm and was swept up to the hotel. He could not remember when he had felt so completely baffled; the incident of the girl and the ceremony was growing to something very like a calamity, and the mystery which surrounded it began to fret him intolerably; and the very unusualness of a trouble he could not settle with his fists whipped his temper to the point of explosion. He caught himself wavering, nevertheless, before the wind-swept porch of the hotel "office." That, too, was strange. Ford was not wont to hesitate before entering a saloon; more often he hesitated about leaving.

"What's the matter with me, anyway?" he questioned himself impatiently. "I'm acting like I hadn't a right to go in and take a drink when I feel like it! If just a slight touch of matrimony acts like that with a man, what can the real thing be like? I always heard it made a fool of a fellow." To prove to himself that he was still untrammeled and at liberty to follow his own desire, he stamped across the porch, threw open the door, and entered with a certain defiance of manner.

Behind the bar, Sam was laughing with his mouth wide open so that his gum showed shamelessly. Bill and Aleck and Big Jim were leaning heavily upon the bar, laughing also.

"I'll bet she's a Heart-and-Hander, tryin' a new scheme to git a man. Think uh nabbing a man when he's drunk. That's a new one," Sam brought his lips close enough together to declare, and chewed vigorously upon the idea, - until he glanced up and saw Ford standing by the door. He turned abruptly, caught up a towel, and began polishing the bar with the frenzy of industry which never imposes upon one in the slightest degree.

Bill glanced behind him and nudged Aleck into

caution, and in the silence which followed, the popping of a piece of slate-veined coal in the stove sounded like a volley of small-caliber pistol shots.

CHAPTER III

ONE WAY TO DROWN SORROW

Ford walked up to the bar, with a smile upon his face which Sam misunderstood and so met with a conciliatory grin and a hand extended toward a certain round, ribbed bottle with a blue-and-silver label. Ford waved away the bottle and leaned, not on the bar but across it, and clutching Sam by the necktie, slapped him first upon one ear and next upon the other, until he was forced by the tingling of his own fingers to desist. By that time Sam's green necktie was pulled tight just under his nose, and he had swallowed his gum - which, considering the size of the lump, was likely to be the death of him.

Ford did not say a word. He permitted Sam to jerk loose and back into a corner, and he watched the swift crimsoning of his ears with a keen interest. Since Sam's face had the pasty pallor of the badly scared, the ears appeared much redder by contrast than they really were. Next, Ford turned his attention to the man beside him, who happened to be Bill. For one long minute the grim spirit of war hovered just over the two.

"Aw, forget it, Ford," Bill urged ingratiatingly at last. "You don't want to lick anybody - least of all old Bill! Look at them knuckles! You couldn't thump a feather bed. Anyway, you got the guilty party when you done slapped Sam up to a peak and then knocked the peak off. Made him swaller his cud, too, by hokey! Say, Sam, my old dad used to feed a cow on bacon-rinds when she done lost her cud. You try it, Sam. Mebby it might help them ears! Shove that there trouble-killer over this way, Sammy, and don't look so fierce at your uncle Bill; he's liable to turn you across his knee and dust your pants proper." He turned again to Ford, scowling at the group and at life in general, while the snow melted upon his broad shoulders and trickled in little, hurrying drops down to the nearest jumping-off place. "Come, drownd your sorrer," Bill advised amiably. "Nobody said nothing but Sammy, and I'll gamble he wishes he hadn't, now." If his counsel was vicious, his smile was engaging - which does not, in this instance, mean that it was beautiful.

Ford's fingers closed upon the bottle, and with reprehensible thoroughness he proceeded to drown what sorrows he then possessed. Unfortunately he straightway produced a fresh supply, after his usual method. In two hours he was flushed and argumentative. In three he had whipped Bill - cause unknown to the chronicler, and somewhat hazy to Ford also after it was all over. By mid-afternoon he had Sammy entrenched in the tiny stronghold where barreled liquors were kept, and scared to the babbling stage. Aleck had been put to bed with a gash over his right eye where Ford had pointed his argument with a beer glass, and Big Jim had succumbed to a billiard cue directed first at his most sensitive bunion and later at his head. Ford was not using his fists, that day, because even in his whisky-brewed rage he remembered, oddly enough, his skinned knuckles.

Others had come - in fact, the entire male population of Sunset was hovering in the immediate vicinity of the hotel - but none had conquered. There had been considerable ducking to avoid painful contact with flying glasses from the bar, and a few had retreated in search of bandages and liniment; the luckier ones remained as near the storm-center as was safe and expostulated. To those Ford had but one reply, which developed into a sort of war-chant, discouraging to the peace-loving listeners.

"I'm a rooting, tooting, shooting, fighting son-of-a-gun - *and a good one!*" Ford would declaim, and with deadly intent aim a lump of coal, billiard ball, or glass at some unfortunate individual in his audience. "Hit the nigger and get a cigar! You're just hanging around out there till I drink myself to sleep - but I'm fooling you a few! I'm watching the clock with one eye, and I take my dose regular and not too frequent. I'm going to kill off a few of these smart boys that have been talking about me and my wife. She's a lady, my wife is, and I'll kill the first man that says she isn't." (One cannot, you will understand, be too explicit in a case like this; not one thousandth part as explicit as Ford was.)

"I'm going to begin on Sam, pretty quick," he called through the open door. "I've got him right where I want him." And he stated, with terrible exactness, his immediate intentions towards the bartender.

Behind his barricade of barrels, Sam heard and shivered like a gun-shy collie at a turkey shoot; shivered until human nerves could bear no more, and like the collie he left the storeroom and fled with a yelp of sheer terror. Ford turned just as Sam shot through the doorway into the dining-room, and splintered a beer bottle against the casing; glanced solemnly up at the barroom clock and, retreating to the nearly denuded bar, gravely poured himself another drink; held up the glass to the dusk-filmed window, squinted through it, decided that he needed a little more than that, and added another teaspoonful. Then he poured the contents of the glass down his throat as if it were so much water, wiped his lips upon a bar towel, picked a handful of coal from the depleted coal-hod, went to the door, and shouted to those outside to produce Sam, that he might be killed in an extremely unpleasant manner.

The group outside withdrew across the street to grapple with the problem before them. It was obviously impossible for civilized men to sacrifice Sam, even if they could catch him - which they could not. Sam had bolted through the dining-room, upset the Chinaman in the kitchen, and fallen over a bucket of ashes in the coal-shed in his flight for freedom. He had not stopped at that, but had scurried off up the railroad track. The general opinion among the spectators was that he had, by this time, reached the next station and was hiding in a cellar there.

Bill Wright hysterically insisted that it was up to Tom Aldershot, who was a deputy town marshal. Tom, however, was working on the house he hoped to have ready for his prospective bride by Thanksgiving, and hated to be interrupted for the sake of a few broken heads only.

"He ain't shooting up nobody," he argued from the platform, where he was doing "inside work" on his dining-room while the storm lasted. "He never does cut loose with his gun when he's drunk. If I arrested him, I'd have to take him clear up to Garbin - and I ain't got time. And it wouldn't be nothin' but a charge uh disturbin' the peace, when I got him there. Y'oughta have a jail in Sunset, like I've been telling yuh right along, Can't expect a man to stop his work just to take a man to jail - not for anything less than murder, anyhow."

Some member of the deputation hinted a doubt of his courage, and Tom flushed.

"I ain't scared of him," he snorted indignantly. "I should say not! I'll go over and make him behave - as a man and a citizen. But I ain't going to arrest him as an officer, when there ain't no place to put him." Tom reluctantly threw down his hammer, grumbling because they would not wait till it was too dark to drive nails, but must cut short his working day, and went over to the hotel to quell Ford.

Ingress by way of the front door was obviously impracticable; the marshal ducked around the corner just in time to avoid a painful meeting with a billiard ball. Mother McGrew had piled two tables against the dining-room door and braced them with the mop, and stubbornly refused to let Tom touch the barricade either as man or officer of the law.

"Well, if I can't get in, I can't do nothing," stated Tom, with philosophic calm.

"He's tearing up the whole place, and he musta found all them extra billiard balls Mike had under the bar, and is throwin' 'em away," wailed Mrs. McGrew, "and he's drinkin' and not payin'. The damage that man is doin' it would take a year's profits to make up. You gotta do something, Tom Aldershot - you that calls yourself a marshal, swore to perfect the citizens uh Sunset! No, sir - I ain't a-goin' to open this door, neither. I'm tryin' to save the dishes, if you want to know. I ain't goin' to let my cups and plates foller the glasses in there. A town full uh men - and you stand back and let one crazy -"

Tom had heard Mrs. McGrew voice her opinion of the male population of Sunset on certain previous occasions. He left her at that point, and went back to the group across the street.

At length Sandy, whose imagination had been developed somewhat beyond the elementary stage by his reading of romantic fiction, suggested luring Ford into the liquor room by the simple method of pretending an assault upon him by way of the storeroom window, which could be barred from without by heavy planks. Secure in his belief in Ford's friendship for him, Sandy even volunteered to slam the door shut upon Ford and lock it with the padlock which guarded the room from robbery. Tom took a chew of tobacco, decided that the ruse might work, and donated the planks for the window.

It did work, up to a certain point. Ford heard a noise in the storeroom and went to investigate, caught a glimpse of Tom Aldershot apparently about to climb through the little window, and hurled a hammer and considerable vituperation at the opening. Whereupon Sandy scuttled in and slammed the door, according to his own plan, and locked it. There was a season of frenzied hammering outside, and after that Sunset breathed freer, and discussed the evils of strong drink, and washed down their arguments by copious draughts of the stuff they maligned.

B. M. Bower

Later, they had to take him out of the storeroom, because he insisted upon knocking the bungs out of all the barrels and letting the liquor flood the floor, and Mike McGrew's wife objected to the waste, on the ground that whisky costs money. They fell upon him in a body, bundled him up, hustled him over to the ice-house, and shut him in; and within ten minutes he kicked three boards off one side and emerged breathing fire and brimstone like the dragons of old. He had forgotten about wanting to kill Sam; he was willing - nay, anxious - to murder every male human in Sunset.

They did not know what to do with him after that. They liked Ford when he was sober, and so they hated to shoot him, though that seemed the only way in which they might dampen his enthusiasm for blood. Tom said that, if he failed to improve in temper by the next day, he would try and land him in jail, though it did seem rigorous treatment for so common a fault as getting drunk. Meanwhile they kept out of his way as well as they could, and dodged missiles and swore. Even that was becoming more and more difficult - except the swearing - because Ford developed a perfectly diabolic tendency to empty every store that contained a man, so that it became no uncommon sight to see a back door belching forth hurrying figures at the most unseasonable times. No man could lift a full glass, that night, and feel sure of drinking the contents undisturbed; whereat Sunset grumbled while it dodged.

It may have been nine o'clock before the sporadic talk of a jail crystallized into a definite project which, it was unanimously agreed, could not too soon be made a reality.

They built the jail that night, by the light of bonfires which the slightly wounded kept blazing in the intervals of standing guard over the workers; ready to give warning in case Ford appeared as a war-cloud on their horizon. There were fifteen able-bodied men, and they worked fast, with Ford's war-chant in the saloon down the street as an incentive to speed. They erected it close to Tom Aldershot's house, because the town borrowed lumber from him and they wanted to save carrying, and because it was Tom's duty to look after the prisoner, and he wanted the jail handy, so that he need not lose any time from his house-building.

They built it strong, and they built it tight, without any window save a narrow slit near the ceiling; they heated it by setting a stove outside under a shelter, where Tom could keep up the fire without the risk of going inside, and ran pipe and a borrowed "drum" through the jail high enough so that Ford could not kick it. And to discourage any thought of suicide by hanging, they ceiled the place tightly with Tom's matched flooring of Oregon pine. Tom did not like that, and said so; but the citizens of Sunset nailed it on and turned a deaf ear to his complaints.

Chill dawn spread over the town, dulling the light of the fires and bringing into relief the sodden tramplings in the snow around the jail, with the sharply defined paths leading to Tom Aldershot's lumber-pile. The watchers had long before sneaked off to their beds, for not a sign of Ford had they seen since midnight. The storm had ceased early in the evening and all the sky was glowing crimson with the coming glory of the sun. The jail was almost finished. Up on the roof three crouching figures were nailing down strips of brick-red building paper as a fair substitute for shingles, and on

B. M. Bower

the side nearest town the marshal and another were holding a yard-wide piece flat against the wall with fingers that tingled in the cold, while Bill Wright fastened it into place with shingle nails driven through tin disks the size of a half-dollar.

Ford, partly sober after a sleep on the billiard table in the hotel barroom, heard the hammering, wondered what industrious soul was up and doing carpenter work at that unseemly hour, and after helping himself to a generous "eye-opener" at the deserted bar, found his cap and went over to investigate. He was much surprised to see Bill Wright working, and smiled to himself as he walked quietly up to him through the soft, step-muffling snow.

"What you doing, Bill - building a chicken house?" he asked, a quirk of amusement at the corner of his lips.

Bill jumped and came near swallowing a nail; so near that his eyes bulged at the feel of it next his palate. Tom Aldershot dropped his end of the strip of paper, which tore with a dull sound of ripping, and remarked that he would be damned. Necks craned, up on the roof, and startled eyes peered down like chipmunks from a tree. Some one up there dropped a hammer which hit Bill on the head, but no one said a word.

"You act like you were nervous, this morning," Ford observed, in the tone which indicates a conscious effort at good-humored ignorance. "Working on a bet, or what?"

"What!" snarled Bill sarcastically. "I wisht, Ford, next time you bowl up, you'd pick on somebody that ain't too good a friend to fight back! I'm gittin' tired, by hokey -"

"What - did I lick you again, Bill?" Ford's smile was sympathetic to a degree. "That's too bad, now. Next time you want to hunt a hole and crawl into it, Bill. I don't want to hurt you - but seems like I've kinda got the habit. You'll have to excuse me." He hunched his shoulders at the chill of the morning and walked around the jail, inspecting it with half-hearted interest.

"What is this, anyway?" he inquired of Tom. "Smoke-house?"

"It's a jail," snapped Tom. "To put you into if you don't watch your dodgers. What 'n thunder you want to carry on like you did last night, for? And then go and sober up just when we've got a jail built to put you into! That ain't no way for a man to do - I'll leave it to Bill if it is! I've a darned good mind to swear out a warrant, anyway, Ford, and pinch you for disturbin' the peace! That's what I ought to do, all right." Tom beat his hands about his body and glared at Ford with his ultra-official scowl.

"All right, if you want to do it." Ford's tone embellished the reply with a you-take-the-conse-quences sort of indifference. "Only, I'd advise you never to turn me loose again if you do lock me up in this coop once."

"I know I wouldn't uh worked all night on the thing if I'd knowed you was goin' to sleep it off," Bill complained, with deep reproach in his watery eyes. "I made sure you was due to keep things agitated around here for a couple uh days, at the very least, or I never woulda drove a nail, by hokey!"

"It is a darned shame, to have a nice, new jail and nobody to use it on," sympathized Ford, his eyes half-closed and steely. "I'd like to help you out, all right. Maybe I'd better kill you, Bill; they *might* stretch a point and call it manslaughter - and I could use the bounty to help pay a lawyer, if it ever come to a head as a trial."

Whereat Bill almost wept.

Ford pushed his hands deep into his pockets and walked away, sneering openly at Bill, the marshal, the jail, and the town which owned it, and at wives and matrimony and the world which held all these vexations.

He went straight to the shack, drank a cup of coffee, and packed everything he could find that belonged to him and was not too large for easy carrying on horseback; and when Sandy, hovering uneasily around him, asked questions, he told him briefly to go off in a corner and lie down; which advice Sandy understood as an invitation to mind his own affairs.

Like Bill, Sandy could have wept at the ingratitude of this man. But he asked no more questions and he made no more objections. He picked up the story of the unpronounceable count who owned the castle in the Black Forest and had much tribulation and no joy until the last chapter, and when Ford went out, with his battered, sole-leather suitcase and his rifle in its pigskin case, he kept his pale eyes upon his book and refused even a grunt in response to Ford's grudging: "So long, Sandy."

CHAPTER IV

REACTION

Even when a man consistently takes Life in twenty-four-hour doses and likes those doses full-flavored with the joys of this earth, there are intervals when the soul of him is sick, and Life becomes a nauseous progression of bleak futility. He may, in his revulsion against it, attempt to end it all; he may, in sheer disgust of it, take his doses stronger than ever before, as if he would once for all choke to death that part of him which is fine enough to rebel against it; he may even forswear, in melancholy penitence, that which has served to give it flavor, and vow him vows of abstemiousness at which the grosser part of him chuckles ironically; or, he may blindly follow the first errant impulse for change of environment, in the half-formed hope that new scenes may, without further effort on his part, serve to make of him a new man - a man for whom he can feel some respect.

Ford did none of these things, however. The soul-sick incentive was there, and if he had been a little less of a reasoning animal and a little less sophisticated, he would probably have forsworn strong drink just as he forswore all responsibility for his inadvertent marriage. His reason and his experience saved him from cluttering his conscience with broken vows, although

B. M. Bower

he did yield to the impulse of change to the extent of leaving Sunset while yet the inhabitants were fortifying themselves for the ardors of the day with breakfast and some wild prophecies concerning Ford's next outbreak.

Apprehension over Bill's immediate future was popular amongst his friends, Ford's sardonic reference to manslaughter and bounty being repeated often enough in Bill's presence to keep that peace-loving gentleman in a state of trepidation which he sought to hide behind vague warnings.

"He better think twicet before he comes bothering around me, by hokey!" Bill would mutter darkly. "I've stood a hull lot from Ford; I like 'im, when he's himself. But I've stood about as much as a man can be expected to stand. And he better look out! That's all I got to say - he better look out!" Bill himself, it may be observed incidentally, spent the greater portion of that day in "looking out." He was careful not to sit down with his back to a door, for instance, and was keenly interested when a knob turned beneath unseen fingers, and plainly relieved when another than Ford entered his presence. Bill's mustache was nearly pulled from its roots, that day - but that is not important to the story, which has to do with Ford Campbell, sometime the possessor of a neat legacy in coin, later a rider of the cattle ranges, last presiding genius over the poker table in Scotty's back room in Sunset, always an important factor - and too often a disturbing element - in any community upon which he chose to bestow his dynamic presence.

Scotty hoped that Ford would show up for business when the lamps were lighted, that night. There had been some delicacy on the part of Ford's acquaintances that day in the matter of calling upon him at the shack. They believed - and hoped - that Ford was "sleeping it off," and there was a unanimous reluctance to disturb his slumbers. Sandy, indulging himself in the matter of undisturbed spinal tremors over "The Haunted Chamber," had not left shelter, save when the more insistent shiverings of chilled flesh recalled him from his pleasurable nerve-crimplings and drove him forth to the woodpile. So that it was not until evening was well advanced that Sunset learned that Ford was no longer a potential menace within its meager boundaries. Bill took a long breath, observed meaningly that "He'd *better* go - whilst his credit's good, by hokey!" and for the first time that day sat down with his back toward an outer door.

Ford was not worrying about Sunset half as much as Sunset was worrying about him. He was at that moment playing pinochle half-heartedly with a hospitable sheep-herder, under the impression that, since his host had frankly and profanely professed a revulsion against solitaire and a corresponding hunger for pinochle, his duty as a guest lay in satisfying that hunger. He played apathetically, overlooked several melts he might have made, and so lost three games in succession to the gleeful herder, who had needed the diversion almost as much as he needed a hair-cut.

His sense of social responsibility being eased thereby, Ford took his headache and his dull disgust with life to the wall side of the herder's frowsy bunk, and straightway forgot both in heavy slumber, leaving to the morrow any definite plan for the near future - the far future being as little considered as death and what is said to lie beyond.

B. M. Bower

That day had done for him all he asked of it. It had put him thirty miles and more from Sunset, against which he felt a resentment which it little deserved; of a truth it was as inoffensive a hamlet as any in that region, and its sudden, overweening desire for a jail was but a legitimate impulse toward self-preservation. The fault was Ford's, in harassing the men of Sunset into action. But several times that day, and again while he was pulling the stale-odored blankets snugly about his ears, Ford anathematized the place as "a damned, rotten hole," and was as nearly thankful as his mood would permit, when he remembered that it lay far behind him and was likely to be farther before his journeyings were done.

Sleep held him until daylight seeped in through the one dingy window. Ford awoke to the acrid smell of scorched bacon, thought at first that Sandy was once more demonstrating his inefficiency as a cook, and when he remembered that Sandy's name was printed smudgily upon that page of his life which he had lately turned down as a blotted, unlearned lesson is pushed behind an unwilling schoolboy, he began to consider seriously his next step.

Outside, the sheep were blatting stridently their demand for breakfast. The herder bolted coffee and coarse food until he was filled, and went away to his dreary day's work, telling Ford to make himself at home, and flinging back a hope of further triumphs in pinochle, that night.

Ford washed the dishes, straightened the blankets in the bunk, swept the grimy floor as well as he could with the stub of broom he found, filled the wood-box and then, being face to face with his day and the problem it held, rolled a cigarette, and smoked it in deep meditation.

He wanted to get away from town, and poker games, and whisky, and the tumult it brewed. Something within him hungered for clean, wind-swept reaches and the sane laughter of men, and Ford was accustomed to doing, or at least trying to do, the thing he wanted to do. He was not getting into the wilderness because of any inward struggle toward right living, but because he was sick of town and the sordid life he had lived there.

Somewhere, back toward the rim of mountains which showed a faint violet against the sky to the east, he owned a friend; and that friend owned a stock ranch which, Ford judged, must be of goodly extent; two weeks before, hearing somehow that Ford Campbell was running a poker game in Sunset, the friend had written and asked him to come and take charge of his "outfit," on the plea that, his foreman having died, he was burdened with many cares and in urgent need of help.

Ford, giving the herder's frying-pan a last wipe with the dish-cloth, laughed at the thought of taking the responsibility offered him in that letter. It occurred to him, however, that the Double Cross (which was the brand-name of Mason's ranch) might be a pleasant place to visit. It was long since he had seen Ches - and there had been a time when one bed held the two of them through many a long, weary night; when one frying-pan cooked the scanty food they shared between them. And there had been a season of grinding days and anxious, black nights between, when the one problem, to Ford, consisted of getting Ches Mason out of the wild land where they wandered, and getting him out alive. The problem Ford solved and at the solution men wondered. Afterward they had drifted apart, but the memory of those months would hold them together with a bond which not even time could break - a bond which would pull taut whenever they met.

Ford set down the frying-pan and went to the door and looked out. A chinook had blown up in the night, and although the wind was chill, the snow had disappeared, save where drifts clung to the hollows, shrinking and turning black beneath the sweeping gusts; sodden masses which gave to the prairie a dreary aspect of bleak discomfort. But Ford was well pleased at the sight of the brown, beaten grasses. Impulse was hardening to decision while he stared across the empty land toward the violet rim of hills; a decision to ride over to the Double Cross, and tell Ches Mason to his face that he was a chump, and have a smoke with the old Turk, anyway. Ches had married, since that vividly remembered time when adventure changed to hardship and hazard and walked hand in hand with them through the wild places. Ford wondered fleetingly if matrimony had changed old Ches; probably not - at least, not in those essential man-traits which appeal to men. Ford suddenly hungered for the man's hearty voice, where kindly humor lurked always, and for a grip of his hand.

It was like him to forget all about the herder and the promise of pinochle that night. He went eagerly to the decrepit little shed which housed Rambler, his long-legged, flea-bitten gray; saddled him purposefully and rode away toward the violet hills at the trail-trot which eats up the miles with the least effort.

That night, although he slept in a hamlet which called itself a town, his purpose kept firm hold of him, and he rode away at a decent hour the next morning, - and he rode sober. He kept his face toward the hills, and he did not trouble himself with any useless analysis of his unusual temperateness. He was going to blow in to the Double Cross some time before he slept that night, and have a talk with Ches. He had a pint of fairly good whisky in his pocket, in case he felt the need of a little on the way, and beyond those two satisfactory certainties he did not attempt to reason. They were significant, in a way, to a man with a tendency toward introspection; but Ford was interested in actualities and never stopped to wonder why he bought a pint, rather than a quart, or why, with Ches Mason in his mind, he declined to "set in" to the poker game which was running to tempting jackpots, the night before; or why he took one glass of wine before he mounted Rambler and let it go at that. He never once dreamed that the memory of cheerful, steady-going Ches influenced him toward starting on his friendly pilgrimage the Ford Campbell whom Mason had known eight years before; a very different Ford Campbell, be it said, from the one who had caused a whole town to breathe freer for his absence.

Of his wife Ford had thought less often and less uncomfortably since he left the town wherein had occurred the untoward incident of his marriage. He was not unaccustomed to doing foolish things when he was drunk, and as a rule he made it a point to ignore them afterwards. His mysterious, matrimonial accident was beginning to seem less of a real catastrophe than before, and the anticipation of meeting Ches Mason was rapidly taking precedence of all else in his mind.

So, with almost his normal degree of careless equanimity, he faced again the rim of hills - nearer they were now, with a deeper tinge that was almost purple where the shadows lined them here and there. Somewhere out that way lay the Double Cross ranch. Forty miles, one man told him it was; another, forty-three. At best it was far enough for the shortened daylight of one fall day to cover the journey. Ford threw away the stub of his after-breakfast cigarette and swung into the trail at a lope.

CHAPTER V

"I CAN SPARE THIS PARTICULAR GIRL"

Ford's range-trained vision told him, while yet afar off, that the lone horse feeding upon a side hill was saddled and bridled, with reins dragging; the telltale, upward toss of its head when it started on to find a sweeter morsel was evidence enough of the impeding bridle, even before he was near enough to distinguish the saddle.

Your true range man owns blood-relationship with the original Good Samaritan; Ford swung out of the trail and untied his rope as a matter of course. The master of the animal might have turned him loose to feed, but if that were the case, he had strayed farther than was ever intended; the chances, since no human being was in sight, were all against design and in favor of accident. At any rate Ford did not hesitate. It is not good to let a horse run loose upon the range with a saddle cinched upon its back, as every one knows.

Ford was riding along the sheer edge of a water-worn gully, seeking a place where he might safely jump it - or better, a spot where the banks sloped so that he might ride down into it and climb the bank beyond - when he saw a head and pair of shoulders moving slowly along, just over the brow of the hill where fed

B. M. Bower

the stray. He watched, and when the figure topped the ridge and started down the slope which faced him, his eyes widened a trifle in surprise.

Skirts to the tops of her shoes betrayed her a woman. She limped painfully, so that Ford immediately pictured to himself puckered eyebrows and lips pressed tightly together. "And I'll bet she's crying, too," he summed up aloud. While he was speaking, she stumbled and fell headlong.

When he saw that she made no attempt to rise, but lay still just as she had fallen, Ford looked no longer for an easy crossing. He glanced up and down the washout, saw no more promising point than where he was, wheeled and rode back twenty yards or so, turned and drove deep his spurs.

It was a nasty jump, and he knew it all along. When Rambler rose gamely to it, with tensed muscles and forefeet flung forward to catch the bank beyond, he knew it better. And when, after a sickening minute of frenzied scrambling at the crumbling edge, they slid helplessly to the bottom, he cursed his idiocy for ever attempting it.

Rambler got up with a pronounced limp, but Ford had thrown himself from the saddle and escaped with nothing worse than a skinned elbow. They were penned, however, in a box-like gully ten feet deep, and there was nothing to do but follow it to where they might climb out. Ford was worried about the girl, and made a futile attempt to stand in the saddle and from there climb up to the level. But Rambler, lame as he was, plunged so that Ford finally gave it up and started down the gulch, leading Rambler by the reins.

There were many sharp turns and temper-trying windings, and though it narrowed in many places so that there was barely room for them to pass, it never grew shallower; indeed, it grew always deeper; and then, without any warning, it stopped abruptly upon a coulee's rim, with jumbled rocks and between them a sheer descent to the slope below. Ford guessed then that he was boxed up in one of the main waterways of the foot-hills he had been skirting for the past hour or so, and that he should have ridden up the gulch instead of down it.

He turned, though the place was so narrow that Rambler's four feet almost touched one another and his rump scraped the bank, as Ford pulled him round, and retraced his steps. It was too rough for riding, even if he had not wanted to save the horse, and he had no idea how far he must go before he could get out. Ford, at that time, was not particularly cheerful.

He must have gone a mile and more before he reached the point where, by hard scrambling, he attained level ground upon the same side as the girl. Ten minutes he spent in urging Rambler up the bank, and when the horse stood breathing heavily beside him, Ford knew that, for all the good there was in him at present, he might as well have left him at the bottom. He walked around him, rubbing leg and shoulder muscles until he located the hurt, and shook his head when all was done. Then he started on slowly, with Rambler hobbling painfully after him. Ford knew that every rod would aggravate that strained shoulder and that a stop would probably make it impossible for the horse to go on at all.

He was not quite sure, after all those windings where

he could not see, just where it was he had seen the girl, but he recognized at last the undulating outline of the ridge over which she had appeared, and made what haste he could up the slope. The grazing horse was no longer in sight, though he knew it might be feeding in a hollow near by.

He had almost given up hope of finding her, when he turned his head and saw her off to one side, lying half concealed by a clump of low rose bushes. She was not unconscious, as he had thought, but was crying silently, with her face upon her folded arms and her hat askew over one ear. He stooped and touched her upon the shoulder.

She lifted her head and looked at him, and drew away with a faint, withdrawing gesture, which was very slight in itself but none the less eloquent and unmistakable. Ford backed a step when he saw it and closed his lips without speaking the words he had meant to say.

"Well, what do you want?" the girl asked ungraciously, after a minute spent in fumbling unseen hairpins and in straightening her hat. "I don't know why you're standing there like that, staring at me. I don't need any help."

"Appearances are deceitful, then," Ford retorted. "I saw you limping over the hill, after your horse, and I saw you fall down and stay down. I had an idea that a little help would be acceptable, but of course -"

"That was an hour ago," she interrupted accusingly, with a measuring glance at the sun, which was settling toward the sky-line.

"I had trouble getting across that washout down there. I don't know this part of the country, and I went down it instead of up. What are you crying about - if you don't need any help?"

She eyed him askance, and chewed upon a corner of her lip, and flipped the upturned hem of her riding skirt down over one spurred foot with a truly feminine instinct, before she answered him. She seemed to be thinking hard and fast, and she hesitated even while she spoke. Ford wondered at the latent antagonism in her manner.

"I was crying because my foot hurts so and because I don't see how I'm going to get back to the ranch. I suppose they'll hunt me up if I stay away long enough - but it's getting toward night, and - I'm scared to death of coyotes, if you must know!"

Ford laughed - at her defiance, in the face of her absolute helplessness, more than at what she said. "And you tell me you don't need any help?" he bantered.

"I might borrow your horse," she suggested coldly, as if she grudged yielding even that much to circumstance. "Or you might catch mine for me, I suppose."

"Sure. But you needn't hate me because you're in trouble," he hinted irrelevantly. "I'm not to blame, you know."

"I - I hate to ask help from - a stranger," she said, watching him from under her lashes. "And I can't help showing what I feel. I hate to feel under an obligation -"

"If that's all, forget it," he assured her calmly. "It's a law of the open - to help a fellow out in a pinch. When I headed for here, I thought it was a man had been set afoot."

She eyed him curiously. "Then you didn't know -"

"I thought you were a man," he repeated. "I didn't come just because I saw it was a girl. You needn't feel under any obligation whatever. I'm a stranger in the country and a stranger to you. I'm perfectly willing to stay that way, if you prefer. I'm not trying to scrape acquaintance on the strength of your being in trouble; but you surely don't expect a man to ride on and leave a woman out here on the bald prairie - do you? Especially when she's confessed she's afraid of the dark - and coyotes!"

She was staring at him while he spoke, and she continued to stare after he had finished; the introspective look which sees without seeing, it became at last, and Ford gave a shrug at her apparent obstinacy and turned away to where Rambler stood with his head drooped and his eyes half closed. He picked up the reins and chirped to him, and the horse hesitated, swung his left foot painfully forward, hobbled a step, and looked at Ford reproachfully.

"Your horse is crippled as badly as I am, it would seem," the girl observed, from where she sat watching them.

"I strained his shoulder, trying to make him jump that washout. That was when I first got sight of you over here. We went to the bottom and it took me quite a while to find a way out. That's why I was so long getting here." Ford explained indifferently, with his back to her, while he rubbed commiseratingly the swelling shoulder.

"Oh." The girl waited. "It seems to me you need help yourself. I don't see how you expect to help any one else, with your horse in that condition," she added. And when he still did not speak, she asked: "Do you know how far it is to the nearest ranch?"

"No. I told you I'm a stranger in this country. I was heading for the Double Cross, but I don't know just -"

"We're eight miles, straight across, from there; ten, the way we would have to go to get there. There are other washouts in this country - which it is unwise to attempt jumping, Mr. -"

"Campbell," Ford supplied shortly.

"I beg your pardon? You mumbled -"

"Campbell!" Ford was tempted to shout it but contented himself with a tart distinctness. A late, untoward incident had made him somewhat touchy over his name, and he had not mumbled.

"Oh. Did you skin your face and blacken your eye, Mr. Campbell, when you tried to jump that washout?"

"No." Ford did not offer any explanation. He remembered the scars of battle which were still plainly visible upon his countenance, and he turned red while he bent over the fore ankles of Rambler, trying to discover other sprains. He felt that he was going to dislike this girl very much before he succeeded in getting her to shelter. He could not remember ever meeting before a woman under forty with so unpleasant a manner and with such a talent for disagreeable utterances.

"Then you must have been fighting a wildcat," she hazarded.

"Pardon me; is this a Methodist experience meeting?" he retorted, looking full at her with lowering brows. "It seems to me the only subject which concerns us mutually is the problem of getting to a ranch before dark."

"You'll have to solve it yourself. I never attempt puzzles." The girl, somewhat to his surprise, showed no resentment at his rebuff. Indeed, he began to suspect her of being secretly amused. He began also mentally to accuse her of not being too badly hurt to walk, if she wanted to; indeed, his skepticism went so far as to accuse her of deliberately baiting him - though why, he did not try to conjecture. Women were queer. Witness his own late experience with one.

Being thus in a finely soured mood, Ford suggested that, as she no doubt knew the shortest way to the nearest ranch, they at least make a start in that direction.

"How?" asked the girl, staring up at him from where she sat beside the rose bushes.

"By walking, I suppose - unless you expect me to carry you." Ford's tone was not in any degree affable.

"I fancy it would be asking too great a favor to suggest that you catch my horse for me?"

Ford dropped Rambler's reins and turned to her, irritated to the point where he felt a distinct desire to shake her.

"I'd far rather catch your horse, even if I had to haze him all over the country, than carry you," he stated bluntly.

"Yes. I suspected that much." She had plucked a red seed-ball off the bush nearest her and was nibbling daintily the sweet pulp off the outside.

"Where is the horse?" Ford was holding himself rigidly hack from an outburst of temper.

"Oh, I don't know, I'm sure." She picked another seed-ball and began upon it. "He should be somewhere around, unless he has taken a notion to go home."

Ford said something under his breath and untied his rope from the saddle. He knew about where the horse had been feeding when he saw him, and he judged that it would naturally graze in the direction of home - which would probably be somewhere off to the southeast, since the trail ran more or less in that direction. Without a word to the girl, or a glance toward her, he started up the hill, hoping to get his bearings and a sight of the horse from the top. He could not remember when he had been so angry with a woman. "If she was a man," he gritted as he climbed, "I'd give her a thrashing or leave her out there, just as she deserves. That's the worst of dealing with a woman - she can always hand it to you, and you've got to give her a grin and thank-you, because she ain't a man."

He glanced back, then, and saw her sitting with her

head dropped forward upon her hands. There was something infinitely pitiful and lonely in her attitude, and he knitted his brows over the contrast between it and her manner when he left her. "I don't suppose a woman knows, herself, what she means, half the time," he hazarded impatiently. "She certainly didn't have any excuse for throwing it into me the way she did; maybe she's sorry for it now."

After that his anger cooled imperceptibly, and he hurried a little faster because the day was waning with the chill haste of mid-autumn, and he recalled what she had said at first about being afraid of coyotes. And, although the storm of three days ago had been swept into mere memory by that sudden chinook wind, and the days were once more invitingly warm and hazily tranquil, night came shiveringly upon the land and the unhoused thought longingly of hot suppers and the glow of a fire.

The girl's horse was, he believed, just disappearing into a deep depression half a mile farther on; but when he reached the place where he had seen it, there was nothing in sight save a few head of cattle and a coyote trotting leisurely up the farther slope. He went farther down the shallow coulee, then up to the high level beyond, his rope coiled loosely over one arm with the end dragging a foot behind him. But there was nothing to be seen from up there, except that the sun was just a red disk upon the far-off hills, and that the night was going to be uncomfortably cool if that wind kept blowing from the northwest.

He began to feel slightly uneasy about the girl, and to regret wasting any time over her horse, and to fear that he might not be able to get close enough to rope the beast, even if he did see him.

He turned back then and walked swiftly through the dusk toward the ridge, beyond which she and Rambler were waiting. But it was a long way - much farther than he had realized until he came to retrace his steps - and the wind blew up a thin rift of clouds which made the darkness come quickly. He found it difficult to tell exactly at which point he had crossed the ridge, coming over; and although experience in the open develops in a man a certain animal instinct for directions handed down by our primitive ancestry, Ford went wide in his anxiety to take the shortest way back to his unwilling protegee. The westering slope was lighter, however, and five minutes of wandering along the ridge showed him a dim bulk which he knew was Rambler. He hurried to the place, and the horse whinnied shrilly as he approached.

"I looked as long as I could see, almost, but I couldn't locate your horse," Ford remarked to the dark shadow of the rose bushes. "I'll put you on mine. It will be slow going, of course - lame as he is - but I guess we can manage to get somewhere."

He waited for the chill, impersonal reply. When she did not speak, he leaned and peered at the spot where he knew she must be. "If you want to try it, we'd better be starting," he urged sharply. "It's going to be pretty cold here on this side-hill."

When there was silence still - and he gave her plenty of time for reply - Ford stooped and felt gropingly for her, thinking she must be asleep. He glanced back at Rambler; unless the horse had moved, she should have been just there, under his hands; or, he thought, she

B. M. Bower

may have moved to some other spot, and be waiting in the dark to see what he would do. His palms touched the pressed grasses where she had been, but he did not say a word. He would not give her that satisfaction; and he told himself grimly that he had his opinion of a girl who would waste time in foolery, out here in the cold - with a sprained ankle, to boot.

He pulled a handful of the long grass which grows best among bushes. It was dead now, and dry. He twisted it into a makeshift torch, lighted and held it high, so that its blaze made a great disk of brightness all around him. While it burned he looked for her, and when it grew to black cinders and was near to scorching his hand, he made another and looked farther. He laid aside his dignity and called, and while his voice went booming full-lunged through the whispering silence of that empty land, he twisted the third torch, and stamped the embers of the second into the earth that it might not fire the prairie.

There was no dodging the fact; the girl was gone. When Ford was perfectly sure of it, he stamped the third torch to death with vicious heels, went back to the horse, and urged him to limp up the hill. He did not say anything then or think anything much; at least, he did not think coherently. He was so full of a wordless rage against the girl, that he did not at first feel the need of expression. She had made a fool of him.

He remembered once shooting a big, beautiful, blacktail doe. She had dropped limply in her tracks and lain there, and he had sauntered up and stood looking at her stretched before him. He was out of meat, and the doe meant all that hot venison steaks and rich, brown gravy can mean to a man meat-hungry. While he unsheathed his hunting knife, he gloated over the feast he would have, that night. And just when he had laid his rifle against a rock and knelt to bleed her, the deer leaped from under his hand and bounded away over the hill. He had not said a word on that occasion, either.

This night, although the case was altogether different and the disappearance of the girl was in no sense a disaster - rather a relief, if anything - he felt that same wordless rage, the same sense of utter chagrin. She had made a fool of him. After awhile he felt his jaws aching with the vicelike pressure of his teeth together.

They topped the ridge, Rambler hobbling stiffly. Ford had in mind a sheltering rim of sandstone at the nearest point of the coulee he had crossed in searching for the girl's horse, and made for it. He had noticed a spring there, and while the water might not be good, the shelter would be welcome, at any rate.

He had the saddle off Rambler, the shoulder bathed with cold water from the spring, and was warming his wet hands over a little fire when the first gleam of humor struck through his anger and lighted for a moment the situation.

"Lordy me! I must be a hoodoo, where women are concerned," he said, kicking the smoking stub of a bush into the blaze. "Soon as one crosses my trail, she goes and disappears off the face of the earth!" He fumbled for his tobacco and papers. It was a "dry camp" he was making that night, and a smoke would have to serve for a supper. He held his book of papers absently while he stared hard at the fire.

"It ain't such a bad hoodoo," he mused. "I can spare this particular girl just as easy as not; and the other one, too, for that matter."

After a minute spent in blowing apart the thin leaves and selecting a paper:

"Queer where she got to - and it's a darned mean trick to play on a man that was just trying to help her out of a fix. Why, I wouldn't treat a stray dog that way! Darn these women!"

CHAPTER VI

THE PROBLEM OF GETTING SOMEWHERE

Dawn came tardily after a long, cheerless night, during which the wind whined over the prairie and the stars showed dimly through a shifting veil of low-sweeping clouds. Ford had not slept much, for hunger and cold make poor bedfellows, and all the brush he could glean on that barren hillside, with the added warmth of his saddle-blanket wrapped about him, could no more make him comfortable than could cigarettes still the gnawing of his hunger.

When he could see across the coulee, he rose from where he had been sitting with his back to the ledge and his feet to the meager fire, brooding over all the unpleasant elements in his life thus far, particularly the feminine element. He folded the saddle-blanket along its original creases and went over to where Rambler stood dispiritedly with his back humped to the cold, creeping wind and his tail whipping between his legs when a sudden gust played with it. Ford shivered, and beat his gloved hands about his body, and looked up at the sky to see whether the sun would presently shine and send a little warmth to this bleak land where he wandered. He blamed the girl for all of this discomfort, and he told himself that the next time a woman appeared within his range of vision he would ride way

B. M. Bower

around her. They invariably brought trouble; of various sorts and degrees, it is true, but trouble always. It was perfectly safe, he decided, to bank on that. And he wished, more than ever, that he had not improvidently given that pint of whisky to a disconsolate-looking sheep-herder he had met the day before on his way out from town; or that he had put two flasks in his pocket instead of one. In his opinion a good, big jolt right now would make a new man of him.

Rambler, as he had half expected, was obliged to do his walking with three legs only; which is awkward for a horse accustomed to four exceedingly limber ones, and does not make for speed, however great one's hurry. Ford walked around him twice, scooped water in his hands, and once more bathed the shoulder - not that he had any great faith in cold water as a liniment, but because there was nothing else that he could do, and his anxiety and his pity impelled service of some sort. He rubbed until his fingers were numb and his arm aching, tried him again, and gave up all hope of leading the horse to a ranch. A mile he might manage, if he had to but ten! He rubbed Rambler's nose commiseratingly, straightened his forelock, told him over and over that it was a darned shame, anyway, and finally turned to pick up his saddle. He could not leave that lying on the prairie for inquisitive kit-foxes to chew into shoestrings, however much he might dread the forty-pound burden of it on his shoulders. He was stooping to pick it up when he saw a bit of paper twisted and tied to the saddle-horn with a red ribbon.

"Lordy me!" he ejaculated ironically. "The lady left a note on my pillow - and I never received it in time! Now, ain't that a darned shame?" He plucked the knot loose, and held up the ribbon and the note, and laughed.

"'When this reaches you, I shall be far away, though it breaks my heart to go and this missive is mussed up scandalous with my bitter tears. Forgive me if you can, and forget me if you have to. It is better thus, for it couldn't otherwise was,'" he improvised mockingly, while his chilled fingers fumbled to release the paper, which was evidently a leaf torn from a man's memorandum book. "Lordy me, a letter from a lady! Ain't that sweet!"

When he read it, however, the smile vanished with a click of the teeth which betrayed his returning anger. One cold, curt sentence bidding him wait until help came - that was all. His eye measured accusingly the wide margin left blank under the words; she had not omitted apology or explanation for lack of space, at any rate. His face grew cynically amused again.

"Oh, certainly! I'd roost on this side-hill for a month, if a lady told me to," he sneered, speaking aloud as he frequently did in the solitude of the range land. He glanced from ribbon to note, ended his indecision by stuffing the note carelessly into his coat pocket and letting the ribbon drop to the ground, and with a curl of the lips which betrayed his mental attitude toward all women and particularly toward that woman, picked up his saddle.

"I can't seem to recollect asking that lady for help, anyway," he summed up before he dismissed the subject from his mind altogether. "I was trying to help her; it sure takes a woman to twist things around so they point backwards!"

He turned and glanced pityingly at Rambler, watching him with ears perked forward inquiringly. "And I crippled a damned good horse trying to help a blamed poor specimen of a woman!" he gritted. "And didn't get so much as a pleasant word for it. I'll sure remember that!"

Rambler whinnied after him wistfully, and Ford set his teeth hard together and walked the faster, his shoulders slightly bent under the weight of the saddle. His own physical discomfort was nothing, beside the hurt of leaving his horse out there practically helpless; for a moment his fingers rested upon the butt of his six-shooter, while he considered going back and putting an end to life and misery for Rambler. But for all the hardness men had found in Ford Campbell, he was woman-weak where his horse was concerned. With cold reason urging him, he laid the saddle on the ground and went back, his hand clutching grimly the gun at his hip. Rambler's nicker of welcome stopped him half-way and held him there, hot with guilt.

"Oh, damn it, I can't!" he muttered savagely, and retraced his steps to where the saddle lay. After that he almost trotted down the coulee, and he would not look back again until it struck him as odd that the nickerings of the horse did not grow perceptibly fainter. With a queer gripping of the muscles in his throat he did turn, then, and saw Rambler's head over the little ridge he had just crossed. The horse was making shift to follow him rather than be left alone in that strange country. Ford waited, his lashes glistening in the first rays of the new-risen sun, until the horse came hobbling stiffly up to him.

"You old devil!" he murmured then, his contrite tone

contrasting oddly with the words he used. "You contrary, ornery, old devil, you!" he repeated softly, rubbing the speckled nose with more affection than he had ever shown a woman. "You'd tag along, if - if you didn't have but one leg to carry you! And I was going to -" He could not bring himself to confess his meditated deed of mercy; it seemed black-hearted treachery, now, and he stood ashamed and humbled before the dumb brute that nuzzled him with such implicit faith.

It was slow journeying, after that. Ford carried the saddle on his own back rather than burden the horse with it, and hungry as he was, he stopped often and long, and massaged the sprained shoulder faithfully while Rambler rested it, with all his weight on his other legs and his nose rooting gently at Ford's bowed head.

A stray rider assured him that he was on the right trail, but it was past noon when he thankfully reached the Double Cross, threw his saddle down beside the stable door, and gave Rambler a chance at the hay in the corral.

B. M. Bower

CHAPTER VII

THE FOREMAN OF THE DOUBLE CROSS

"Hell-o, Ford, where the blazes did you drop down from?" a welcoming voice yelled, when he was closing the gate of the corral behind him and thinking that it was like Ches Mason to have a fine, strong corral and gate, and then slur the details by using a piece of baling wire to fasten it. The last ounce of disgust with life slid from his mind when he heard the greeting, and he turned and gripped hard the gloved hand thrust toward him. Ches Mason it was - the same old Ches, with the same humorous wrinkles around his eyes and mouth, the same kindliness, the same hearty faith in the world as he knew it and in his fellowmen as he found them - the unquestioning faith that takes it for granted that the other fellow is as square as himself. Ford held his hand while he permitted himself a swift, reckoning glance which took in these familiar landmarks of the other's personality.

"Don't seem to have hurt you much - matrimony," he observed whimsically, as he dropped the hand. "You look just like you always did - with your hat on." In the West, not to say in every other locality, there is a time-honored joke about matrimony, for certain strenuous reasons, producing premature baldness.

Ches grinned and removed his hat. Eight years had heightened his forehead perceptibly and thinned the hair on his temples. "You see what it's done to me," he pointed out lugubriously. "You ain't married yourself, I suppose? You look like you'd met up with some kinda misfortune." Mason was regarding Ford's scarred face with some solicitude.

"Just got tangled up a little with my fellow-citizens, in Sunset," Ford explained drily. "I tried to see how much of the real stuff I could get outside of, and then how many I could lick." He shrugged his shoulders a little. "I did quite a lot of both," he added, as an afterthought.

Mason was rubbing his jaw reflectively and staring hard at Ford. "The wife's strong on the temperance dope," he said hesitatingly. "I reckon you'll want to bunk down with the boys till you grow some hide on your face - there's lady company up at the house, and -"

"The bunk-house for mine, then," Ford cut in hastily. "No lady can get within gunshot of me; not if I see her coming in time!" Though he smiled when he said it, there was meaning behind the mirth.

Mason pulled a splinter from a corral rail and began to snap off little bits with his fingers. "Kate will go straight up in the air with me if she knows you're here and won't come to the house, though," he considered uneasily. "She's kept a big package of gratitude tucked away with your name on it, ever since that Alaska deal. And lemme tell you, Ford, when a woman as good as Kate goes and gets grateful to a man - gosh! Had your dinner?"

B. M. Bower

"Not lately, I haven't," Ford declared. "I kinda remember eating, some time in the past; it was a long time ago, though."

Mason laughed and tagged the answer as being the natural exaggeration of a hungry man. "Well, come along and eat, then - if you haven't forgotten how to make your jaws go. I've got Mose Freeman cooking for me; you know Mose, don't you? Hired him the day after the Fourth; the Mitten outfit fired him for getting soused and trying to clean out the camp, and I nabbed him before they had time to forgive him. Way they had of disciplining him - when he'd go on a big tear they'd fire him for a few days and then take him back. But they can't git him now - not if I can help it. A better cook never throwed dishwater over a guy-rope than that same old Mose, but -" He stopped and looked at Ford hesitantly. "Say! I hate like the deuce to tie a string on you as soon as you hit the ranch, Ford, but - if you've got anything along, you won't spring it on Mose, will you? A fellow's got to watch him pretty close, or -"

"I haven't got a drop." Ford's tone was reprehensibly regretful.

"You do look as if you'd put it all under your belt," Mason retorted dryly. "Left anything behind?"

"Some spoiled beauties, and a nice new jail that was built by my admiring townspeople, with my name carved over the door. I didn't stay for the dedication services. Sunset was getting all fussed up over me and I thought I'd give them a chance to settle their nerves; loss of sleep sure plays hell with folks when their nerves are getting frazzly." He smiled disarmingly at Mason.

"I'd kinda lost track of you, Ches, till I got your letter. I've been traveling pretty swift, and that's no lie. I meant to write, but - you know how a man gets to putting things off. And then I took a notion to ride over this way, and sample your grub for a day or so, and abuse you a little to your face, you old highbinder!"

"Sure. I've been kinda looking for you, too. But - I wish you hadn't quite so big an assortment of battle-signs, Ford. Kate's got ideals and prejudices - and she don't know all your little personal traits. She's heard a lot about you, of course. We was married right after we came outa the North, you know, and of course - Well, you know how a woman sops up adventure stories; and seeing you was the star performer -"

"And that's a lie," Ford put in modestly, albeit a trifle bluntly.

"No, it ain't. She got the truth. And she's so darned grateful," he added lugubriously, "that I don't know how to square your record with that face! Unless we can rig up some yarn about a holdup - " He paused just outside the mess-house door and eyed Ford questioningly. "We might -"

"No, you don't. If you've gone and lied to her, and made me out a little tin angel, you deserve what's coming. Anyway, I won't stay long, and I'll stop down here with the boys. Call me Jack Jones and let it go at that. Honest, Ches, I don't want to get mixed up with no more females. I'm plumb scared of 'em. Lordy me, that coffee sure does smell good to me!"

Mason looked at him doubtfully, saw that Ford was, for the time being, absolutely devoid of anything remotely approaching penitence for his sins, or compunction over his appearance, or uneasiness over "Kate's" opinion of him. He was hungry. And since it is next to impossible to whip up the conscience of a man whose thoughts are concentrated upon his physical needs, Mason was wise enough to wait, though the one point which he considered of vital importance to them both - the question of Ford's acceptance or refusal of the foremanship of the Double Cross - had not yet been touched upon.

While Ford ate with a controlled voraciousness which spoke eloquently of his twenty-four hours of fasting and exposure, Mason gossiped inattentively and studied the man.

Eight years leave their impress of mental growth or deterioration upon a man. Outwardly Ford was not much changed since Mason had come with him out of Alaska and lost sight of him afterwards. There was the maturity which the man of thirty possessed and which the virile young fellow of twenty-one had lacked. There was the same straight glance, the same atmosphere of squareness and mental poise. Those were qualities which Mason set down as valuable factors in his estimate of the man. Besides, there were other signs which did not make so pleasant a reading.

Eight years - and a few of them, at least, had been spent wastefully in tearing down what the other years had built; Mason had heard that Ford was "going to the dogs," and that by the short trail men blazed for themselves centuries ago and which those who came after have made a highway - the whisky trail. Mason had heard, now and then, of ten thousand dollars coming to Ford upon the death of his father and going almost as suddenly as it had come. That, at least, had been the rumor. Also he had heard, just lately, that Ford had taken to gambling as a profession and to terrorizing Sunset periodically as a pastime. And Mason remembered the Ford Campbell who had carried him on his back out of a wild place in Alaska, and had nearly starved himself that the sick man's strength might not fail him utterly. He had remembered - had Ches Mason; and, being one of those tenacious souls who cling to friendship and to a resilient faith in the good that is in the worst of us, he had thrown out a tentative life-line, as it were, and hoped that Ford might clutch it before he became quite submerged in the sodden morass of inebriety.

Ford may or may not have grasped eagerly at the line. At any rate he was there in the mess-house of the Double Cross, and he was not quite so sodden as Mason had feared to find him - provided he found him at all. So much, at least, was encouraging, and for the rest, Mason was content to wait.

Mose, recognizing Ford at once, had asked him, with a comical attempt at secrecy, if he had anything to drink. When Ford shook his head, Mose stifled a sigh and went back to his dishwashing, not more than half convinced and inclined toward resentfulness. That a "booze-fighter" like Ford Campbell should come only a day's ride from town and not be fairly well supplied with whisky was too remarkable to be altogether plausible. He eyed the two sourly while they talked, and he did not bring forth one of the fresh pies he had baked, as he had meant to do.

B. M. Bower

It was not until Ford was ready to light his after-dinner cigarette that Mason led the way into the next room, which held the bunks and general belongings of the men, and closed the door so that they might talk in confidence without fear of Mose's loose tongue. Ford immediately pulled off his boots, laid himself down upon one of the bunks, doubled a pillow under his head, and began to eye Mason quizzically. Then he said:

"Say, you kinda played your hand face down, didn't you, Ches, when you wrote and asked me to come out here and take charge? Eight years is a long time to expect a man to stay right where he was when you saw him last. You've lost a whole lot of horse sense since I knew you."

"Well, what about it? You came, I notice." Mason grinned and would not help Ford otherwise to an understanding.

"I didn't come to hog-tie that foreman job, you chump. I just merely want to tell you that you'll get into all kinds of trouble, some day, if you go laying yourself wide open like that. Why, it's plumb crazy to offer a job like that to a fellow you haven't seen for as long as you have me. And if you heard anything about me, it's a cinch it wasn't what would recommend me to any Sunday-school as a teacher of their Bible class! How did you know I wouldn't take it? And let you in for -"

"Well, you're here, and I've seen you. The job's still waiting for you. You can start right in, to-morrow morning." Ches got out his pipe and began to fill it as calmly and with as much attention to the small details as if he were not mentally tensed for the struggle he knew was coming; a struggle which struck much deeper than the position he was offering Ford.

Ford almost dropped his cigarette in his astonishment. "Well, you damn' fool!" he ejaculated pityingly.

"Why? I thought you knew enough - you punched cows for the Circle for four or five years, didn't you? Nelson told me you were his top hand while you stayed with him, and that you ran the outfit one whole summer, when -"

"That ain't the point." A hot look had crept into Ford's face - a tinge which was not a flush - and a glow into his eyes. "I know the cow-business, far as that goes. It's me; you can't - why, Lordy me! You ought to be sent to Sulphur Springs and get your think-tank hoed out. Any man that will offer a foreman's job to a - a -"

"'A rooting, tooting, shooting, fighting son-of-a-gun, and a good one!'" assisted Mason equably. "'The only original go-getter - ' Sure. That's all right."

The flush came slowly and darkened Ford's cheeks and brow and throat. He threw his half-smoked cigarette savagely at the hearth of the rusty box-stove, and scowled at the place where it fell. "Well, ain't that reason enough?" he demanded harshly, after a minute.

Mason had been studying that flush. He nodded assent to some question he had put to himself, and crowded tobacco into his pipe. "No reason at all, one way or the other. I need a foreman - one I can depend on. I've got to make a trip out to the Coast, this fall, and I've got to leave somebody here I can trust."

Ford shot him a quick, questioning glance, and bit his lip. "That," he said more calmly, "is just what I'm driving at. You can't trust me. You can't depend on me, Ches."

"Oh, yes I can," Mason contradicted blandly. "It's just because I can that I want you."

"You can't. You know damn' well you can't! Why, you - don't you know I've got the name of being a drunkard, and a - a bad actor all around? I'm not like I was eight years ago, remember. I've traveled a hard old trail since we bucked the snow together, Ches - and it's been mostly down grade. I was all right for awhile, and then I got ten thousand dollars, and it seemed a lot of money. I bought a fellow out - he had a ranch and a few head of horses - so he could take his wife back East to her mother. She was sick. I didn't want the darned ranch. And so help me, Ches, that's the only thing I've done in the last four years that I hadn't ought to be ashamed of. The rest of the money I just simply blew. I - well, you see me; you didn't want to take me up to the house to meet your wife, and I don't blame you. You'd be a chump if you did. And this is nothing out of the ordinary. I've got my face bunged up half the time, seems like." He thumped the pillow into a different position, settled his head against it, and looked at Mason with his old, whimsical smile. "So when you talk about that foreman job, and depending on me, you're - plumb delirious. I was going to write and tell you so, but I kept putting it off. And then I took a notion I'd hunt you up and give you some good advice. You're a good fellow, Ches, but the court ought to appoint a guardian for you."

"I'll stick around for three or four weeks," Mason

observed, in the casual tone of one who is merely discussing the details of an everyday affair, "till the calves are all gathered. We're a little late this year, on account of old Slow dying right in round-up time. We got most of the beef shipped - all I care about gathering, this fall. I've got most all young stock, and it won't hurt to let 'em run another season; there ain't many. I'll let you take the wagons out, and I'll go with you till you get kinda harness-broke. And -"

"I told you I don't want the job." Ford's mouth was set grimly.

"You tried to tell me what I want and what I don't want," Mason corrected amiably. "Now I've got my own ideas on that subject. This here outfit belongs to me. I like to pick my men to suit myself; and if I want a certain man for foreman, I guess I've got a right to hire him - if he'll let himself be hired. I've picked my man. It don't make any difference to me how many times he played hookey when he was a kid, or how many men he's licked since he growed up. I've hired him to help run the Double Cross, and run it right; and I ain't a bit afraid but what he'll make good." He smiled and knocked the ashes gently from his pipe into the palm of his hand, because the pipe was a meerschaum just getting a fine, fawn coloring around the base of the bowl, and was dear to the heart of him. "Down to the last, white chip," he added slowly, "he'll make good. He ain't the kind of a man that will lay down on his job." He got up and yawned, elaborately casual in his manner.

"You lay around and take it easy this afternoon," he said. "I've got to jog over to the river field; the boys are over there, working a little bunch we threw in yesterday. To-morrow we can ride around a little, and kinda get the lay of the land. You better go by-low, right now - you look as if it wouldn't do you any harm!" Whereupon he wisely took himself off and left Ford alone.

The door he pulled shut after him closed upon a mental battle-ground. Ford did not go "by-low." Instead, he rolled over and lay with his face upon his folded arms, alive to the finger-tips; alive and fighting. For there are times when the soul of a man awakes and demands a reckoning, and reviews pitilessly the past and faces the future with the veil of illusion torn quite away - and does it whether the man will or no.

CHAPTER VIII

"I WISH YOU'D QUIT BELIEVING IN ME!"

A distant screaming roused Ford from his bitter mood of introspection. He raised his head and listened, his heavy-lidded eyes staring blankly at the wall opposite, before he sprang off the bunk, pulled on his boots, and rushed from the room. Outside, he hesitated long enough to discover which direction he must take to reach the woman who was screaming inarticulately, her voice vibrant with sheer terror. The sound came from the little, brown cottage that seemed trying modestly to hide behind a dispirited row of young cottonwoods across a deep, narrow gully, and he ran headlong toward it. He crossed the plank footbridge in a couple of long leaps, vaulted over the gate which barred his way, and so reached the house just as a woman whom he knew must be Mason's "Kate," jerked open the door and screamed "Chester!" almost in his face. Behind her rolled a puff of slaty blue smoke.

Ford pushed past her in the doorway without speaking; the smoke told its own urgent tale and made words superfluous. She turned and followed him, choking over the pungent smoke.

"Oh, where's Chester?" she wailed. "The whole garret's on fire - and I can't carry Phenie - and she's asleep and

B. M. Bower

can't walk anyway!" She rushed half across the room and stopped, pointing toward a closed door, with Ford at her heels.

"She's in there!" she cried tragically. "Save her, quick - and I'll find Chester. You'd think, with all the men there are on this ranch, there'd be some one around - oh, and my new piano!"

She ran out of the house, scolding hysterically because the men were gone, and Ford laughed a little as he went to the door she had indicated. When his fingers touched the knob, it turned fumblingly under another hand than his own; the door opened, and he confronted the girl whom he had tried to befriend the day before. She had evidently just gotten out of bed, and into a flimsy blue kimono, which she was holding together at the throat with one hand, while with the other she steadied herself against the wall. She stared blankly into his eyes, and her face was very white indeed, with her hair falling thickly upon either side in two braids which reached to her hips.

Ford gave her one quick, startled glance, said "Come on," quite brusquely, and gathered her into his arms with as little sentiment as he would have bestowed upon the piano. His eyes smarted with the smoke, which blinded him so that he bumped into chairs on his way to the door. Outside he stopped, and looked down at the girl, wondering what he should do with her. Since Kate had stated emphatically that she could not walk, it seemed scarcely merciful to deposit her on the ground and leave her to her own devices. She had closed her eyes, and she looked unpleasantly like a corpse; and there was an insistent crackling up in the roof, which warned Ford that there was little time for the weighing of fine points. He was about to lay her on the bare ground, for want of a better place, when he glimpsed Mose running heavily across the bridge, and went hurriedly to meet him.

"Here! You take her down and put her in one of the bunks, Mose," he commanded, when Mose confronted him, panting a good deal because of his two hundred and fifty pounds of excess fat and a pair of down-at-the-heel slippers which hampered his movements appreciably. Mose looked at the girl and then at his two hands.

"I can't take her," he lamented. "I got m'hands full of aigs!"

Ford's reply was a sweep of the girl's inert figure against Mose's outstretched hands, which freed them effectually of their burden of eggs. "You darned chump, what's eggs in a case like this?" he cried sharply, and forced the girl into his arms. "You take her and put her on a bunk. I've got to put out that fire!"

So Mose, a reluctant knight and an awkward one, carried the girl to the bunk-house, and left Ford free to save the house if he could. Fortunately the fire had started in a barrel of old clothing which had stood too close to the stovepipe, and while the smoke was stifling, the flames were as yet purely local. And, more fortunately still, that day happened to be Mrs. Mason's wash-day and two tubs of water stood in the kitchen, close to the narrow stairway which led into the loft. Three or four pails of water and some quick work in running up and down the stairs was all that was needed. Ford, standing in the low, unfinished loft, looked at the rafter which was burnt half through, and wiped his perspiring face with his coat sleeve.

"Lordy me!" he observed aloud, "I sure didn't come any too soon!"

"Oh, it's all out! I don't know how I ever shall thank you in this world! With Phenie in bed with a sprained ankle so she couldn't walk, and the men all gone, I was just wild! I - why - " Kate, standing upon the stairs so that she could look into the loft, stopped suddenly and stared at Ford with some astonishment. Plainly, she had but then discovered that he was a stranger - and it was quite as plain that she was taking stock of his blackened eyes and other bruises, and that with the sheltered woman's usual tendency to exaggerate the disfigurements.

"That's all right; I don't need any thanks." Ford, seeing no other way of escape, approached her steadily, the empty bucket swinging in his hand. "The fire's all out, so there's nothing more I can do here, I guess."

"Oh, but you'll have to bring Josephine back!" Kate's eyes met his straightforward glance reluctantly, and not without reason; for Ford had dark, greenish purple areas in the region of his eyes, a skinned cheek, and a swollen lip; his chin was scratched and there was a bruise on his forehead where, on the night of his marri- age, he had hit the floor violently under the impact of two or three struggling male humans. Although they were five days old - six, some of them - these divers battle-signs were perfectly visible, not to say conspic- uous; so that Kate Mason was perhaps justified in her perfectly apparent diffidence in looking at him. So do we turn our eyes self-consciously away from a cripple, lest we give offense by gazing upon his misfortune.

"*I* can't carry her, and she can't walk - her ankle is sprained dreadfully. So if you'll bring her back to the house, I'll be ever so much -"

"Certainly; I'll bring her back right away." Ford came down the stairs so swiftly that she retreated in haste before him, and once down he did not linger; indeed, he almost ran from the house and from her embarrassed gratitude. On the way to the bunk-house it occurred to him that it might be no easy matter, now, for Mason to conceal Ford's identity and his sins. From the way in which she had stared wincingly at his battered countenance, he realized that she did, indeed, have ideals. Ford grinned to himself, wondering if Ches didn't have to do his smoking altogether in the bunk-house; he judged her to be just the woman to wage a war on tobacco, and swearing, and muddy boots, and drinking out of one's saucer, and all other weaknesses peculiar to the male of our species. He was inclined to pity Ches, in spite of his mental acknowledgment that she was a very nice woman indeed; and he was half inclined to tell Mason when he saw him that he'd have to look further for a foreman.

He found the girl lying upon a bunk just inside the door, still with closed eyes and that corpse-like look in her face. He was guilty of hoping that she would remain in that oblivious state for at least five minutes longer, but the hope was short-lived; for when he lifted her carefully in his arms, her eyes flew open and stared up at him intently.

Ford shut his lips grimly and tried not to mind that unwinking gaze while he carried her out and up the path, across the little bridge and on to the house, and deposited her gently upon her own bed. He had not spoken a word, nor had she. So he left her thankfully to Kate's tearful ministrations and hurried from the room.

"Lordy me!" he sighed, as he closed the door upon them and went back to the bunk-house, which he entered with a sigh of relief. One tribute he paid her, and one only: the tribute of feeling perturbed over her presence, and of going hot all over at the memory of her steady stare into his face. She was a queer girl, he told himself; but then, so far as he had discovered, all women were queer; the only difference being that some women were more so than others.

He sat down on the bunk where she had lain, and speedily forgot the girl and the incident in facing the problem of that foremanship. He could not get away from the conviction that he was not to be trusted. He did not trust himself, and there was no reason why any man who knew him at all should trust him. Ches Mason was a good fellow; he meant well, Ford decided, but he simply did not realize what he was up against. He meant, therefore, to enlighten him further, and go his way. He was almost sorry that he had come.

Mason, when Ford confronted him later at the corral and bluntly stated his view of the matter, heard him through without a word, and did not laugh the issue out of the way, as he had been inclined to do before.

"I'll be all right for a month, maybe," Ford finished, "and that's as long as I can bank on myself. I tell you straight, Ches, it won't work. You may think you're hiring the same fellow that came out of the North with you - but you aren't. Why, damn it, there ain't a man I know that wouldn't give you the laugh if they knew the offer you've made me! They would, that's a fact.

They'd laugh at you. You're all right, Ches, but I won't stand for a deal like that. I can't make good."

Mason waited until he was through. Then he came closer and put both hands on Ford's shoulders, so that they stood face to face, and he looked straight into Ford's discolored eyes with his own shining a little behind their encircling wrinkles.

"You can make good!" he said calmly. "I know it. All you need is a chance to pull up. Seeing you won't give yourself one, I'm giving it to you. You'll do for me what you won't do for yourself, Ford - and if there's a yellow streak in you, I never got a glimpse of it; and the yellow will sure come to the surface of a man when he's bucking a proposition like you and me bucked for two months. You didn't lay down on that job, and you were just a kid, you might say. Gosh, Ford, I'd bank on you any old time - put you on your mettle, and I would! You can make good here - and damn it, you will!"

"I wish I was as sure of that as you seem to be," Ford muttered uneasily, and turned away. Mason's easy chuckle followed him, and Ford swung about and faced him again.

"I haven't made any cast-iron promise -"

"Did I ask you to make any?" Mason's voice sharpened.

"But - Lordy me, Ches! How do you know I -"

"I know. That's enough."

B. M. Bower

"But - maybe I don't want the darned job. I never said -"

Mason was studying him, as a man studies the moods of an untamed horse. "I didn't think you'd dodge," he drawled, and the blood surged answeringly to Ford's cheeks. "You do want it."

"If I should happen to get jagged up in good shape, about the first thing I'd do would be to lick the stuffing out of you for being such a simple-minded cuss," Ford prophesied grimly, as one who knows well whereof he speaks.

"Ye-es - but you won't get jagged."

"Oh, Lord! I wish you'd quit believing in me! You used to have some sense," Ford grumbled. But he reached out and clenched his fingers upon Mason's arm so tight that Mason set his teeth, and he looked at him long, as if there was much that he would like to put into words and could not. "Say! You're white clear down to your toes, Ches," he said finally, and walked away hurriedly with his hat jerked low over his eyes.

Mason looked after him as long as he was in sight, and afterwards took off his hat, and wiped beads of perspiration from his forehead. "Gosh!" he whispered fervently. "That was nip and tuck - but I got him, thank the Lord!" Whereupon he blew his nose violently, and went up to his supper with his hands in his pockets and his humorous lips pursed into a whistle.

Before long he was back, chuckling to himself as he bore down upon Ford in the corral, where he was industriously rubbing Rambler's sprained shoulder with liniment.

"The wife says you've got to come up to the house," he announced gleefully. "You've gone and done the heroic again, and she wants to do something to show her gratitude."

"You go back and tell your wife that I'm a bold, bad man and I won't come." Ford, to prove his sincerity, sat down upon the stout manger there, and crossed his legs with an air of finality.

"I did tell her," Mason confessed sheepishly. "She wanted to know who you was, and I told her before I thought. And she wanted to know what was the matter with your face, 'poor fellow,' and I told her that, too - as near as I knew it. I told her," he stated sweepingly, "that you'd been on a big jamboree and had licked fourteen men hand-running. There ain't," he confided with a twinkle, "any use at all in trying to keep a secret from your wife; not," he qualified, "from a wife like Kate! So she knows the whole darned thing, and she's sore as the deuce because I didn't bring you up to the house right away when you came. She thinks you're sufferin' from them wounds and she's going to doctor 'em. That's the way with a woman - you never can tell what angle she's going to look at a thing from. You're the man that packed me down out of the Wrangel mountains on your back, and that's enough for her - dang it, Kate thinks a lot of me! Besides, you done the heroic this afternoon. You've got to come."

"There ain't anything heroic in sloshing a few buckets of water on a barrel of burning rags," Ford belittled, seeking in his pockets for his cigarette papers.

"How about rescuing a lady?" Mason twitted. "You come along. I want you up there myself. Gosh! I want somebody I can talk to about something besides dresses and the proper way to cure sprained ankles, and whether the grocer sent out the right brand of canned peaches. Women are all right - but a man wants some one around to talk to. You ain't married!"

"Oh. Ain't I?" Ford snorted. "And what if I ain't?"

"Say, there's a mighty nice girl staying with us; the one you rescued. She's laid up now - got bucked off, or fell off, or something yesterday, and hurt her foot - but she's a peach, all right. You'll -"

"I know the lady," Ford cut in dryly. "I met her yesterday, and we commenced hating each other as soon as we got in talking distance. She sent me to catch her horse, and then she pulled out before I got back. She's a peach, all right!"

"Oh. You're the fellow!" Mason regarded him attentively. "Now, I don't believe she said a word to Kate about that, and she must have known who it was packed her out of the house. I wonder why she didn't say anything about it to Kate! But she wasn't to blame for leaving you out there, honest she wasn't. I went out to hunt her up - Kate got kinda worried about her - and she told me about you, and we did wait a little while. But it was getting cold, and she was hurt pretty bad and getting kinda wobbly, so I put her on my horse and brought her home. But she left a note for you, and I sent a man back after you with a horse. He come back and said he couldn't locate you. So we thought you'd gone to some other ranch." He stopped and looked quizzically at Ford. "So you're the man! And you're both here for the winter - at least, Kate says she's going to keep her all winter. Gosh! This is getting romantic!"

"Don't you believe it!" Ford urged emphatically. "I don't want to bump into her again; a little of her company will last me a long while!"

"Oh, you won't meet Jo to-night; Josephine, her name is. She's in bed, and will be for a week or so, most likely. You've just got to come, Ford. Kate'll be down here after you herself, if I go back without you - and she'll give me the dickens into the bargain. I want you to get acquainted with my kid - Buddy. He's down in the river field with the boys, but he'll be back directly. Greatest kid you ever saw, Ford! Only seven, and he can ride like a son-of-a-gun, and wears chaps and spurs, and can sling a loop pretty good, for a little kid! Come on!"

"Wel-ll, all right - but Lordy me! I do hate to, Ches, and that's a fact. Women I'm plumb scared of. I never met one in my life that didn't hand me a package of trouble so big I couldn't see around it. Why -" He shut his teeth upon the impulse to confide to Mason his matrimonial mischance.

"These two won't. My wife's the real goods, once you get to know her; a little fussy, maybe, over some things - most all women are. But she's all right, you bet. And Josephine's the proper stuff too. A little abrupt, maybe -"

"Abrupt!" Ford echoed, and laughed over the word. "Yes, she is what you might call a little - abrupt!"

CHAPTER IX

IMPRESSIONS

Josephine waited languidly while Kate chose a second-best cushion from the couch and, lifting the bandaged foot as gently as might be, placed it, with many little pats and pulls, under the afflicted member. Josephine screwed her lips into a soundless expression of pain, smiled afterwards when Kate glanced at her commiseratingly, and pulled a long, dark-brown braid forward over her chest.

"Do you want tea, Phenie? - or would you rather have chocolate to-day? I can make chocolate just as easy as not; I think I shall, anyway. Buddy is so fond of it and -"

"Is that man here yet?" Josephine's tone carried the full weight of her dislike of him.

"I don't know why you call him 'that man,' the way you do," Kate complained, turning her mind from the momentous decision between tea and chocolate. "Ford's simply fine! Chester thinks there's no one like him; and Buddy just tags him around everywhere. You can always," asserted Kate, with the positiveness of the person who accepts unquestioningly the beliefs of others, living by faith rather than reason, "depend upon the likes and dislikes of children and dogs, you know."

"Has the swelling gone out of his eyes?" Josephine inquired pointedly, with the irrelevance which seemed habitual to her and Kate when they conversed.

"Phenie, I don't think it's kind of you to harp on that. Yes, it has, if you want to know. He's positively handsome - or will be when the - when his nose heals perfectly. And I don't think that's anything one should hold against Ford; it seems narrow, dear."

"The skinned place?" Josephine's tone was perfectly innocent, and her fingers were busy with the wide, black bow which becomingly tied the end of the braid.

"Phenie! If you hadn't a sprained ankle, and weren't such a dear in every other respect, I'd shake you! It isn't fair. Because Ford was pounced upon by a lot of men - sixteen, Chester told me -"

"I suppose he counted the dead after the battle, and told Ches truthfully -"

"Phenie, that sounds catty! When you get down on a man, you're perfectly unmerciful, and Ford doesn't deserve it. You shouldn't judge men by the narrow, Eastern standards. I know it's awful for a man to drink and fight. But Ford wasn't altogether to blame. They got him to drinking and," she went on with her voice lowered to the pitch at which women are wont to relate horrid, immoral things, " - I wouldn't be surprised if they put something in it! Such things are done; I've heard of men being drugged and robbed and all sorts of things. And I'm just as much of an advocate for temperance as you are, Phenie - and I think Ford was

B. M. Bower

just right to fight those men. There are," she declared wisely, "circumstances where it's perfectly just and right for a man to fight. I can imagine circumstances under which Chester would be justified in fighting -"

"In case sixteen men should hold his nose and pour drugged whisky down his throat?" Phenie inquired mildly, curling the end of her braid over a slim forefinger.

Mrs. Kate made an inarticulate sound which might almost be termed a snort, and walked from the room with her head well up and a manner which silently made plain to the onlooker that she might say many things which would effectually crush her opponent, but was magnanimously refraining from doing so.

Josephine did not even pay her the tribute of looking at her; she had at that moment heard a step upon the porch, and she was leaning to one side so that she might see who was coming into the dining-room. As it happened, it was Mason himself. Miss Josephine immediately lost interest in the arrival and took to tracing with her finger the outline of a Japanese lady with a startling coiffure and an immense bow upon her spine, who was simpering at a lotus bed on Josephine's kimono. She did not look up until some one stepped upon the porch again.

This time it was Ford, and he stopped and painstakingly removed the last bit of soil from his boot-soles upon the iron scraper which was attached to one end of the top step; when that duty had been performed, he paid further tribute to the immaculate house he was about to enter, by wiping his feet upon a mat placed with mathematical precision upon the porch, at the head of the steps. Josephine watched the ceremonial, and studied Ford's profile, and did not lay her head back upon the cushion behind her until he disappeared into the dining-room. Then she stared at a colored-crayon portrait of Buddy which hung on the wall opposite, and her eyes were the eyes of one who sees into the past.

Buddy, when he opened the door and projected himself into the room, startled her into a little exclamation.

"Dad says he'll carry you out to the table and you can have a whole side to yourself," he announced without preface. "They'll just pick up your chair, and pack chair and all in, and set you down as ee-asy - do you want to eat out there with us?"

Josephine hesitated for two seconds. "All right," she consented then, in a supremely indifferent tone which was of course quite wasted on Buddy, who immediately disappeared with a whoop.

"Come on, dad - she says yes, all right, she'll come," he announced gleefully. Buddy was Josephine's devoted admirer, at this point in their rather brief acquaintance; which, according to his mother's well-known theory, was convincing proof of her intrinsic worth - Mrs. Kate having frequently strengthened her championship of Ford to his detractor, Miss Josephine, by pointing out that Buddy was fond of him.

Josephine spent the brief interval in tucking back locks of hair and in rearranging the folds of her long, Japanese kimono, and managed to fall into a languidly indifferent attitude by the time Chester opened the door. Behind him came Ford; Miss Josephine moved

　　　　B. M. Bower

her lips and tilted her head in a perfunctory greeting, and afterward gave him no more attention than if he had been a Pullman porter assisting with her suitcases. For the matter of that, she gave quite as much attention as she received from him - and Mason's lips twitched betrayingly at the spectacle.

Through dinner they seemed mutually agreed upon ignoring each other as much as was politely possible, which caused Mason to watch them with amusement, and afterwards relieve his feelings by talking about them to Kate in the kitchen.

"Gosh! Jo and Ford are sure putting up a good bluff," he chuckled, while he selected the freshest dish towel from the rack behind the pantry door. "They'd be sticking out their tongues at each other if they was twenty years younger; pity they ain't, too; it would be a relief to 'em both!"

"Phenie provokes me almost past endurance!" Mrs. Kate complained, burying two plump forearms in a dishpan of sudsy hot water, and bringing up a handful of silver. "It's because Ford had been fighting when he came here, and she knows he has been slightly addicted to liquor. She looks down on him, and I don't think it's fair. If a man wants to reform, I believe in helping him instead of pushing him father down." (Mrs. Kate had certain little peculiarities of speech; one was an italicized delivery, and another was the omission of an r now and then. She always said "father" when she really meant "farther.") "There's a lot that one can do to help. I believe in showing trust and confidence in a man, when he's trying to live down past mistakes. I think it was just fine of you to make him foreman here! If Phenie would only be nice to him, instead of turning up her nose the way she does! You see yourself how she treats Ford, and I just think it's a shame! I think he's just splendid!"

"She don't treat him any worse than he does her," observed Mason, just to the core. "Seems to me, if I was single, and a girl as pretty as Jo -"

"Well, I'm glad Ford has got spunk enough not to care," Mrs. Kate interposed hastily. "Phenie's pretty, of course - but it takes more than that to attract a man like Ford. You can't expect him to like her when she won't look at him, hardly; it makes me feel terribly, because he's sure to think it's because he - I've tried to make her see that it isn't right to condemn a man because he has made one mistake. He ought to be encouraged, instead of being made to feel that he is a - an outcast, practically. And -"

"Jo don't like Ford, because she's stuck on Dick," stated a shrill, positive young voice behind them, and Mrs. Kate turned sharply upon her offspring. "They was waving hands to each other just now, through the window. I seen 'em," Buddy finished complacently. "Dick was down fixing the bridge, and -"

"Buddy, you run right out and play! You must not listen to older people and try to talk about some-thing you don't understand."

"Aw, I understand them two being stuck on each other," Buddy maintained loftily. "And I seen Dick -"

"Chase yourself outdoors, like your mother said; and don't butt in on -"

"Chester!" reproved Mrs. Kate, waving Buddy out of the kitchen. "How can you expect the child to learn good English, when you talk to him like that? Run along, Buddy, and play like a good boy." She gave him a little cake to accelerate his departure and to turn his mind from further argument, and after he was gone she swung the discussion to Buddy and his growing tendency toward grappling with problems beyond his seven years. Also, she pointed out the necessity for choosing one's language carefully in his presence.

Mason, therefore, finished wiping the dishes almost in silence, and left the house as soon as he was through, with the feeling that women were not by nature intended to be really companionable. He had, for instance, been struck with the humorous side of Ford and Josephine's perfectly ridiculous antipathy, and had lingered in the kitchen because of a half-conscious impulse to enjoy the joke with some one. And Mrs. Kate had not taken the view-point which appealed to him, but had been self-consciously virtuous in her determination to lend Ford a helping hand, and resentful because Josephine failed to feel also the urge of uplifting mankind.

Mason, poor man, was vaguely nettled; he did not see that Ford needed any settlement-worker encouragement. If he was let alone, and his moral regeneration forgotten, and he himself treated just like any other man, Mason felt that Ford would thereby have all the encouragement he needed. Ford was once more plainly content with life, and was taking it in twenty-four-hour doses again; healthful doses, these, and different in every respect from those days spent in the sordid round of ill-living in town; nor did he flay his soul with doubts lest he should disappoint this man who trusted him so rashly and so implicitly. Ford was busy at work which appealed to the best of him. He was thrown into companionship with men who perforce lived cleanly and naturally, and with Ches Mason, who was his friend. At meals he sometimes gave thought to Mrs. Kate, and frequently to Josephine. The first he admired impersonally for her housewifely skill, and smiled at secretly for her purely feminine outlook upon life and her positive views upon subjects of which she knew not half the alphabet. He had discovered that Mason did indeed refrain from smoking in the house because she discountenanced tobacco; and since she had a talent for making a man uncomfortably aware of her disapproval by certain wordless manifestations of scorn for his weaknesses, Ford also took to throwing away his cigarette before he crossed the bridge on his way to her domain. He did not, however, go so far as Ches, who kept his tobacco, pipe, and cigarette papers in the stable, and was always borrowing "the makings" from his men.

Ford also followed Mason's example in sterilizing his vocabulary whenever he crossed that boundary between the masculine and feminine element on the ranch, the bridge. Mrs. Kate did not approve of slang. Ford found himself carefully eliminating from his speech certain grammatical inaccuracies in her presence, and would not so much as split an infinitive if he remembered in time. It was trying, to be sure. Ford thanked God that he still retained a smattering of the rules he had reluctantly memorized in school, and that he was not married (at least, not uncomfortably so), and that he was not compelled to do more than eat his meals in the house. Mrs. Kate was a nice woman; Ford would tell any man so in perfect sincerity. He even considered her nice looking, with her smooth, brown hair which was never disordered, her fine, clear skin, her white teeth, her clear blue eyes, and her immaculate shirt-waists. But she was not a comfortable woman to be with; an ordinary human wearied of adjusting his speech, his manners, and his morals to her standard of propriety. Ford, quietly studying matrimony from the well-ordered example before him, began to congratulate himself upon not being able to locate his own wife - since accident had afflicted him with one. When he stopped, during these first busy days at the Double Cross, to think deeply or seriously upon the mysterious entanglement he had fallen into, he was inclined to the opinion that he had had a narrow escape. The woman might have remained in Sunset - and Ford flinched at the thought.

As to Josephine, Ford's thoughts dwelt with her oftener than they did with Mrs. Kate. The thought of her roused a certain resentment which bordered closely upon dislike. Still, she piqued his interest; for a week she was invisible to him, yet her presence in the house created a tangible atmosphere which he felt but could not explain. His first sight of her - beyond a fleeting glimpse once or twice through the window - had been that day when he had helped Mason carry her and her big chair into the dining-room. The brief contact had left with him a vision of the delicate parting in her soft, brown hair, and of long, thick lashes which curled daintily up from the shadow they made on her cheeks. He did not remember ever having seen a woman with such eyelashes. They impelled him to glance at her oftener than he would otherwise have done, and to wonder, now and then, if they did not make her eyes seem darker than they really were. He thought it strange that he had not noticed her lashes that day when he carried her from the house and back again -

until he remembered that at first his haste had been extreme, and that when he took her from the bunkhouse she had stared at him so that he would not look at her.

He did not know that Ches Mason was observant of his rather frequent glances at her during the meal, and he would have resented Mason's diagnosis of that particular symptom of interest. Ford would, if put to the question, have maintained quite sincerely that he was perfectly indifferent to Josephine, but that she did have remarkable eyelashes, and a man couldn't help looking at them.

After all, Ford's interest was centered chiefly upon his work. They were going to start the wagons out again to gather the calves for weaning, and he was absorbed in the endless details which fall upon the shoulders of the foreman. Even the fascination of a woman's beauty did not follow him much beyond the bridge.

Mason, hurrying from the feminine atmosphere at the house, found him seriously discussing with Buddy the diet and general care of Rambler, who had been moved into a roomy box stall for shelter. Buddy was to have the privilege of filling the manger with hay every morning after breakfast, and every evening just before supper. Upon Buddy also devolved the duty of keeping his drinking tub filled with clean water; and Buddy was making himself as tall as possible during the conference, and was crossing his heart solemnly while he promised, wide-eyed, to keep away from Rambler's heels.

"I never knew him to kick, or offer to; but you stay out of the stall, anyway. You can fill his tub through that hole in the wall. And you let Walt rub him down good every day - you see that he does it, Bud! And when he gets well, I'll let you ride him, maybe. Anyway, I leave him in your care, old-timer. And it's a privilege I wouldn't give every man. I think a heap of this horse." He turned at the sound of footsteps, and lowered an eyelid slowly for Mason's benefit. "Bud's going to have charge of Rambler while we're gone," he explained seriously. "I want to be sure he's in good hands."

The two men watched Buddy's departure for the house, and grinned over the manifest struggle between his haste to tell his mother and Jo, and his sense of importance over the trust.

"A kid of your own makes up for a whole lot," Mason observed abstractedly, reaching up to the narrow shelf where he kept his tobacco. "I wish I had two or three more; they give a man something to work for, and look ahead and plan for."

Ford, studying his face with narrowed eyelids, was more than ever thankful that he was not hampered by matrimony.

CHAPTER X

IN WHICH THE DEMON OPENS
AN EYE AND YAWNS

A storm held the Double Cross wagons in a sheltered place in the hills, ten miles from the little town where Ford had spent a night on his way to the ranch a month before. Mason, taking the inaction as an excuse, rode home to his family and left Ford to his own devices with no compunctions whatever. He should, perhaps, have known better; but he was acting upon his belief that nothing so braces a man as the absolute confidence of his friends, and to have stayed in camp on Ford's account would, according to Mason's code, have been an affront to Ford's manifest determination to "make good."

It is true that neither had mentioned the matter since the day of Ford's arrival at the ranch; men do not, as a rule, harp upon the deeper issues within their lives. For that month, it had been as though the subject of intemperance concerned them as little as the political unrest of a hot-tempered people beyond the equator. They had argued the matter to a more or less satisfactory conclusion, and had let it rest there.

Ford had ridden with him a part of the way, and when they came to a certain fork in the trail, he had sent a

B. M. Bower

whimsically solemn message to Buddy, had pulled the collar of his coat closer together under his chin, and had faced the wind with a clean conscience, and with bowed head and hat pulled low over his brows. There were at least three perfectly valid reasons why Ford should ride into town that day. He wanted heavier socks and a new pair of gloves; he was almost out of tobacco, and wanted to see if he could "pick up" another man so that the hours of night-guarding might not fall so heavily upon the crew. Ford had been standing the last guard himself, for the last week, to relieve the burden a little, and Mason had been urgent on the subject of another man - or two, he suggested, would be better. Ford did his simple shopping, therefore, and then rode up to the first saloon on the one little street, and dismounted with a mind at ease. If idle men were to be found in that town, he would have to look for them in a saloon; a fact which every one took for granted, like the shortening of the days as winter approached.

Perhaps he over-estimated his powers of endurance, or under-estimated the strength of his enemy. Certain it is that he had no intention of drinking whisky when he closed the door upon the chill wind; and yet, he involuntarily walked straight up to the bar. There he stuck. The bartender waited expectantly. When Ford, with a sudden lift of his head, turned away to the stove, the man looked after him curiously.

At the stove Ford debated with himself while he drew off his gloves and held his fingers to the welcome heat which emanated from a red glow where the fire burned hottest within. He had not made any promise to himself or any one else, he remembered. He had simply resolved that he would make good, if it were humanly possible to do so. That, he told himself, did not necessarily mean that he should turn a teetotaler out and out. Taking a drink, when a man was cold and felt the need of it, was not -

At that point in the argument two of his own men entered, stamping noisily upon the threshold. They were laughing, from pure animal satisfaction over the comforts within, rather than at any tangible cause for mirth, and they called to Ford with easy comradeship. Dick Thomas - the Dick whom Buddy had mentioned in connection with Josephine - waved his hand hospitably toward the bar.

"Come on, Campbell," he invited. He may have seen the hesitancy in Ford's face, for he laughed. "I believe in starting on the inside and driving the frost out," he said.

The two poured generously from the bottle which the bartender pushed within easy reach, and Ford watched them. There was a peculiar lift to Dick's upper lip - the lift which comes when scorn is the lever. Ford's eyes hardened a little; he walked over and stood beside Dick, and he took a drink as unemotionally as if it had been water. He ordered another round, threw a coin upon the bar, and walked out. He had rather liked Dick, in an impersonal sort of way, but that half-sneer clung disagreeably to his memory. A man likes to be held the master - be the slave circumstance, danger, an opposing human, or his own appetite; and although Ford was not the type of man who troubles himself much about the opinions of his fellows, it irked him much that Dick or any other man should sneer at him for a weakling.

He went to another saloon, found and hired a cow-puncher strayed up from Valley County, and when Dick came in, a half-hour later, Ford went to the bar and deliberately "called up the house." He had been minded to choose a mineral water then, but he caught Dick's mocking eye upon him, and instead took whisky straight, and stared challengingly at the other over the glass tilted against his lips.

After that, the liquor itself waged relentless war against his good resolutions, so that it did not need the urge of Dick's fancied derision to send him down the trail which the past had made familiar. He sat in to a poker game that was creating a small zone of subdued excitement at the far end of the room, and while he was arranging his stacks of red, white, and blue chips neatly before him, he was unpleasantly conscious of Dick's supercilious smile. Never mind - he was not the first foreman who ever played poker; they all did, when the mood seized them. Ford straightened his shoulders instinctively, in defiance of certain inner misgivings, and pushed forward his ante of two white chips.

Jim Felton came up and stood at his shoulder, watching the game in silence; and although he did not once open his lips except to let an occasional thin ribbon of cigarette smoke drift out and away to mingle with the blue cloud which hung under the ceiling, Ford sensed a certain good-will in his nearness, just as intangibly and yet as surely as he sensed Dick's sardonic amusement at his apparent lapse.

With every bet he made and won he felt that silent approbation behind him; insensibly it steadied Ford and sharpened his instinct for reading the faces of the other players, so that the miniature towers of red chips and blue grew higher until they threatened to topple - whereupon other little towers began to grow up around them. And the men in the saloon began to feel the fascination of his success, so that they grouped themselves about his chair and peered down over his shoulder at the game.

Ford gave them no thought, except a vague satisfaction, now and then, that Jim Felton stuck to his post. Later, when he caught the dealer, a slit-eyed, sallow-skinned fellow with fingers all too nimble, slipping a card from the bottom of the deck, and gave him a resounding slap which sent him and his cards sprawling all over that locality, he should have been more than ever glad that Jim was present.

Jim kept back the gambler's partner and the crowd and gave Ford elbow-room and some moral support, which did its part, in that it prevented any interference with the chastisement Ford was administering.

It was not a fight, properly speaking. The gambler, once Ford had finished cuffing him and stating his opinion of cheating the while, backed away and muttered vague threats and maledictions. Ford gathered together what chips he felt certain were his, and cashed them in with a certain grim insistence of manner which brooked no argument. After that he left the saloon, with Jim close behind him.

"If you're going back to camp now, I reckon I'll ride along," said Jim, at his elbow. "There's just nice time to get there for supper - and I sure don't want to miss flopping my lip over Mose's beefsteak; that yearling we beefed this morning is going to make some fine eating, if you ask me." His tone was absolutely devoid of anything approaching persuasion; it simply took a certain improbable thing as a commonplace fact, and it tilted the balance of Ford's intentions.

He did not go on to the next saloon, as he had started to do, but instead he followed Jim to the livery stable and got his horse, without realizing that Jim had anything to do with the change of impulse. So Ford went to camp, instead of spending the night riotously in town as he would otherwise have done, and contented himself with cursing the game, the gambler who would have given a "crooked deal," the town, and all it contained. A mile out, he would have returned for a bottle of whisky; but Jim said he had enough for two, and put his horse into a lope. Ford, swayed by a blind instinct to stay with the man who seemed friendly, followed the pace he set and so was unconsciously led out of the way of further temptation. And so artfully was he led, that he never once suspected that he did not go of his own accord.

Neither did he suspect that Jim's stumbling and immediate spasm of regretful profanity at the bed-wagon where they unsaddled, was the result of two miles of deep cogitation, and calculated to account plausibly for not being able to produce a full flask upon demand. Jim swore volubly and said he had "busted the bottle" by falling against the wagon wheel; and Ford, for a wonder, believed and did not ask for proof. He muddled around camp for a few indecisive minutes, then rolled himself up like a giant cocoon in his blankets, and slept heavily through the night.

He awoke at daylight, found himself fully clothed and with a craving for whisky which he knew of old, and tried to remember just what had occurred the night before; when he could not recall anything very distinctly, he felt the first twinge of fear that he had known for years.

"Lordy me! I wonder what kinda fool I made of myself, anyway!" he thought distressfully. Later, when he discovered more money in his pockets than his salary would account for, and remembered playing poker, and having an argument of some sort with some one, his distress grew upon him. In reality he had not done anything disgraceful, according to the easy judgment of his fellows; but Ford did not know that, and he flayed himself unmercifully for a spineless, drunken idiot whom no man could respect or trust. It seemed to him that the men eyed him askance; though they were merely envious over his winnings and inclined to admire the manner in which he had shown his disapproval of the dealer's attempt at cheating.

He dreaded Mason's return, and yet he was anxious to see him and tell him, once for all, that he was not to be trusted. He held aloof from Jim and he was scantily civil to Dick Thomas, whose friendship rang false. He pushed the work ahead while the air was still alive with swirls of mote-like snowflakes, and himself bore the brunt of it just to dull that gnawing self-disgust which made his waking hours a mental torment.

Before, when disgust had seized upon him in Sunset, it had been an abstract rebellion against the futility of life as he was living it. This was different: This was a definite, concrete sense of failure to keep faith with himself and with Mason; the sickening consciousness of a swinish return to the wallow; a distrust of himself that was beyond any emotion he had ever felt in his life.

So, for a week of hard work and harder thinking. Mason sent word by a migratory cowboy, who had stopped all night at the ranch and whom he had hired and sent on to camp, that he would not return to the round-up, and that Ford was to go ahead as they had planned. That balked Ford's determination to turn the work over to Mason and leave the country, and, after the first day of inner rebellion, he settled down insensibly to the task before him and let his own peculiar moral problem wait upon his leisure. He did not dream that the cowboy had witnessed his chastisement of the gambler and had gleefully, and in perfect innocence, recounted the incident at the Double Cross ranch, and that Mason had deliberately thrown Ford upon his own resources in obedience to his theory that nothing so braces a man as responsibility.

Ford went about his business with grim industry and a sureness of judgment born of his thorough knowledge of range work. There was the winnowing process which left the bigger, stronger calves in charge of two men, at a line camp known locally as Ten Mile, and took the younger ones on to the home ranch, where hay and shelter were more plentiful and the loss would be correspondingly less.

Not until the last cow of the herd was safe inside the big corral beyond the stables, did Ford relax his vigilance and ride over to where Ches Mason and Buddy were standing in the shelter of the stable, waiting to greet him.

"Good boy!" cried Mason, when Ford dismounted and flung the stirrup up over the saddle, that he might loosen the latigo and free his steaming horse of its burden. "I didn't look for you before to-morrow night, at the earliest. But I'm mighty glad you're here, let me tell you. That leaves me free to hit the trail to-morrow. I've got to make a trip home; the old man's down with inflammatory rheumatism, and they want me to go - haven't been home for six years, so I guess they've got a license to put in a bid for a month or two of my time, huh? I didn't want to pull out, though, till you showed up. I'm kinda leery about leaving the women alone, with just a couple of sow-egians on the ranch. Bud, you go get a pan of oats for old Schley. Supper's about ready, Ford. Have the boys shovel some hay into the corral, and we'll leave the bunch there till morning. Say, the wagons didn't beat you much; they never pulled in till after three. Mose says the going's bad, on them dobe patches."

Not much of an opening, that, for saying what Ford felt he was in duty bound to say. He was constrained to wait until a better opportunity presented itself - and, as is the way with opportunity, it did not seem as if it would ever come of its own accord. There was Buddy, full of exciting anecdotes about Rambler, and how he had rubbed the liniment on, all alone, and Rambler never kicked or did a thing; and how he and Josephine rode clear over to Jenson's and got caught in the storm and almost got lost - only Buddy's horse knew the way home. And, later, there was Mrs. Kate's excellent supper and gracious welcome, and an evening devoted to four-handed cribbage - with Josephine and Mason as implacable adversaries - and a steady undercurrent of latent hostility between him and the girl, which prevented his thinking much about himself and his duty to Mason. There was everything, in fact, to thwart a man's resolution to discharge honorably a disagreeable duty, and to distract his attention.

Ford went to bed with the baffled sense of being placed in a false position against his will; and, man-like, he speedily gave over thinking of that, and permitted his thoughts to dwell upon a certain face which owned a perfectly amazing pair of lashes, and upon a manner tantalizingly aloof, with glimpses now and then of fascinating possibilities in the way of comradeship, when the girl inadvertently lowered her guard in the excitement of close playing.

CHAPTER XI

"IT'S GOING TO BE AN UPHILL CLIMB!"

Ford was no moral weakling except, perhaps, when whisky and he came to hand-grips. He had made up his mind that Mason must be told of his backsliding, and protected from the risk of leaving a drunkard in charge of his ranch. And when he saw that the opportunity for opening the subject easily did not show any sign of presenting itself, he grimly interrupted Mason in the middle of a funny story about Josephine and Buddy and Kate, involving themselves in a three-cornered argument to the complete discomfiture of the women.

"I tell you, Ford, that kid's a corker! Kate's got all kinds of book theories about raising children, but they don't none of 'em work, with Bud. He gets the best of her right along when she starts to reason with him. Gosh! You can't reason with a kid like Bud; you've got to take him on an equal footing, and when he goes too far, just set down on him and no argument about it. Kate's going to have her hands full while I'm gone, if -"

"She sure will, Ches, unless you get somebody here you can depend on," was the way in which Ford made his opportunity. "You've got the idea, somehow, that cutting out whisky is like getting rid of a mean horse.

B. M. Bower

It's something you don't -"

"Oh, don't go worrying over that, no more," Mason expostulated hastily. "Forget it. That's the quickest cure; try Christian Science dope on it. The more you worry about it, the more -"

"But wait till I tell you! That day I went to town, and you came on home, I got drunk as a fool, Ches. I don't know what all I did, but I know -"

"Well, I know - more about it than you do, I reckon," Mason cut in dryly. "I was told five different times, by one stranger and four of these here trouble-peddlin' friends that clutter the country. That's all right, Ford. A little slip like that - " He held out his hand for Ford's sack of tobacco.

"I ain't the least bit uneasy over that, old man. I'm just as sure as I stand here that you're going to pull up, all right."

"I know you are, Ches." Ford's voice was humble. "That's the hell of it. You're more sure than sensible - but - But look at it like I was a stranger, Ches. Just forget you ever knew me when I was kinda half-way decent. You ain't a fool, even if you do act like one. You know what I'm up against. I'm going to put up the damnedest fight I've got in me, but I don't want you to take any gamble on it. Maybe I'll win, and then again maybe I won't. Maybe I'll go down and out. I don't know - I don't feel half as sure of myself as I did before I made that bobble in town. Before that, I did kinda have an idea that all there was to it was to quit. I thought, once I made up my mind, that would settle it. But that's just the commencement; you've got to fight something inside of you that's as husky a fighter as you are. You've got to -"

"There!" Mason reached out and tapped him impressively on the arm with a match he was about to light. "Now you've got the bull right by the horns! You ain't so darned sure of yourself now - and so I'm dead willing to gamble on you. I ain't a bit afraid to go off and let you have full swing."

"Well, I hope you won't feel like kicking me all over the ranch when you get back," Ford said, after a long pause, during which Mason's whole attention seemed centered upon his cigarette. "It's going to be an uphill climb, old-timer - and a blamed long hill at that. And it's going to be pretty darned slippery, in places."

"I sabe that, all right," grinned Mason. "But I sabe you pretty well, too. You'll dig in your toes and hang on by your eye-winkers if you have to. But you'll get up, all right; I'll bank on that.

"Speaking of booze-fighters," he went on, without giving Ford a chance to contradict him, "I wish you'd keep an eye on old Mose. Now, there's a man that'll drink whisky as long as it's made, if he can get it. I wouldn't trust that old devil as far as I can throw him, and that's a fact. I have to watch pretty close, to keep it off the ranch, and him on. It's the only way to get along with him - he's apt to run amuck, if he gets full enough; and good cooks are as scarce as good foremen." A heartening smile went with the last sentence.

"If he does make connections with the booze, don't can him, Ford, if you can help it. Just shut him up

B. M. Bower

somewhere till he gets over it. There's nothing holds good men with an outfit like the right kind of grub - and Mose sure can cook. The rest of the men you can handle to suit yourself. Slim and Johnnie are all right over at Ten Mile - you made a good stab when you picked them two out - and you will want a couple of fellows here besides Walt, to feed them calves. When the cows are throwed back on the range and the fences gone over careful - I ought to have tended to that before, but I got to putting it off - you can pay off what men you don't need or want."

There was no combating the friendship of a man like that. Ford mentally squared his shoulders and set his feet upon the uphill trail.

He realized to the full the tribute Mason paid to his innate trustworthiness by leaving him there, master of the ranch and guardian of his household god - and goddess, to say nothing of Josephine, whom Mason openly admired and looked upon as one of the family.

Of a truth, it would seem that she had really become so. Ford had gathered, bit by bit, the information that she was quite alone in the world, so far as immediate relatives were concerned, and that she was Kate's cousin, and that Kate insisted that this was to be her home, from now on. Josephine's ankle was well enough now so that she was often to be met in unexpected places about the ranch, he discovered. And though she was not friendly, she was less openly antagonistic than she had been - and when all was said and done, eminently able to take care of herself.

So also was Kate, for that matter. No sooner was her beloved Chester out of sight over the hill a mile away, than Mrs. Kate dried her wifely tears and laid hold of her scepter with a firmness that amused Ford exceedingly. She ordered Dick up to work in the depressed-looking area before the house, which she called her flower garden, a task which Dick seemed perfectly willing to perform, by the way - although his assistance would have been more than welcome at other work than tying scraggly rose bushes and protecting them from the winter already at hand.

As to Buddy, he surely would have resented, more keenly than the women, the implication that he needed any one to take care of him. Buddy's allegiance to Ford was wavering, at that time. Dick had gone to some trouble to alter an old pair of chaps so that Buddy could wear them, and his star was in the ascendant; a pair of chaps with fringes were, in Buddy's estimation, a surer pledge of friendship and favor than the privilege of feeding a lame horse.

Buddy was rather terrible, sometimes. He had a way of standing back unnoticed, and of listening when he was believed to be engrossed in his play. Afterward he was apt to say the things which should not be said; in other words, he was the average child of seven, living without playmates, and so forced by his environment to interest himself in the endless drama played by the grown-ups around him. Buddy, therefore, was not unusually startling, one day at dinner, when he looked up from spatting his potato into a flat cake on his plate.

"What hill you going to climb, Ford?" was his manner of exploding his bomb. "Bald pinnacle? I can climb that hill myself."

"I don't know as I'm going to climb any hills at all,"

B. M. Bower

Ford said indulgently, accepting another helping of potato salad from Mrs. Kate.

"You told dad before he went to gran'ma's house you was going to climb a big, long hill, and he was more sure than sensible." He giggled and showed where two front teeth were missing from among their fellows. "Dad told him he'd make it, but he'd have to dig in his toes and hang on by his eye-winkers," he added to the two women. "Gee! I'd like to see Ford hang onto a hill by his eye-winkers. Jo could do it - she's got winkers six feet long."

Miss Josephine had been looking at Ford's face going red, as enlightenment came to him, but when she caught a quick glance leveled at her lashes, she drooped them immediately so that they almost touched her cheeks. Bud gave a squeal and pointed to her with his fork.

"Jo's blushing! I guess she's ashamed because she's got such long winkers, and Ford keeps looking at 'em all the time. Why don't you shave 'em off with dad's razor? Then Ford would like you, maybe. He don't now. He told dad -"

"Robert Chester Mason, do you want me to get the hairbrush?" This, it need not be explained, from Mrs. Kate, in a voice that portended grave disaster.

"I guess we can get along without it, mamma," Buddy answered her, with an ingratiating smile. Even in the first seven years of one's life, one learns the elementary principles of diplomacy. He did not retire from the conversation, but he prudently changed the subject to what he considered a more pleasant channel.

"Dick likes you anyway, Jo," he informed her soothingly. "He likes you, winkers and all. I can tell, all right. When you go out for a ride he gives me nickels if I tell him where -"

"Robert Ches -"

"Oh, all right." Buddy's tone was wearily tolerant. "A man never knows what to talk about to women, anyway. I'd hate to be married to 'em - wouldn't you, Ford?"

"A little boy like you -" began his mother, somewhat pinker of cheeks than usual.

"I guess I'm pretty near a man, now." He turned his eyes to Ford, consciously ignoring the feminine members of his family. "If I had a wife," he stated calmly, "I'd snub her up to a post and then I'd talk to her about anything I damn pleased!"

Mrs. Kate rose up then in all the terrifying dignity of outraged motherhood, grasped Buddy by the wrist, and led him away, in the direction of the hairbrush, if one would judge by Buddy's reluctance to go.

"So you are going to climb the - Big Hill, are you?" Miss Josephine observed, when the two were quite alone. "It is to be hoped, Mr. Campbell, that you won't find it as steep as it looks - from the bottom."

Ford was not an adept at reading what lies underneath the speech of a woman. To himself he accented the last three words, so that they overshadowed all the rest and made her appear to remind him where he stood - at the bottom.

B. M. Bower

"I suppose a hollow does look pretty high, to a man down a well," he retorted, glancing into his teacup because he felt and was resisting an impulse to look at her.

"One can always keep climbing," she murmured, "and never give up -" Miss Josephine, also, was tilting her teacup and looking studiously into it as if she would read her fortune in the specks of tea leaves there.

"Like the frog in the well - that climbed one jump and fell back two!" he interrupted, but she paid no attention, and went on.

"And the reward for reaching the top -"

"Is there supposed to be a reward?" Ford could not tell why he asked her that, nor why he glanced stealthily at her from under his eyebrows as he awaited her reply.

"There - might - there usually is a reward for any great achievement - and -" Miss Josephine was plainly floundering where she had hoped to float airily upon the surface.

"What's the reward for - climbing hills, for instance?" He looked at her full, now, and his lips were ready to smile.

Miss Josephine looked uneasily at the door. "I - really, I never - investigated the matter at all." She gave a twitch of shoulders and met his eyes steadily. "The inner satisfaction of having climbed the hill, I suppose," she said, in the tone of one who has at last reached firm ground. "Will you have more tea, Mr. Campbell?"

Her final words were chilly and impersonal, but Ford left the table, smiling to himself. At the door he met Dick, whom Buddy had mentioned with disaster to himself. Dick saw the smile, and within the room he saw Miss Josephine sitting alone, her chin resting in her two palms and her eyes fixed upon vacancy.

"Hello," Ford greeted somewhat inattentively. "Do you want me for anything, Dick?"

"Can't say I do," drawled Dick, brushing past Ford in the doorway.

Ford hesitated long enough to give him a second glance - an attentive enough glance this time - and went his way; without the smile, however.

"Lordy me!" he said to himself, when his foot touched the bridge, but he did not add anything to the exclamation. He was wondering when it was that he had begun to dislike Dick Thomas; a long while, it seemed to him, though he had never till just now quite realized it, beyond resenting his covert sneer that day in town. He had once or twice since suspected Dick of a certain disappointment that he himself was not foreman of the Double Cross, and once he had asked Mason why he hadn't given the place to Dick.

"Didn't want to," Mason had replied succinctly, and let it go at that.

If Dick cherished any animosity, however, he had not made it manifest in actual hostility. On the contrary, he had shown a distinct inclination to be friendly; a friendliness which led the two to pair off frequently when they were riding, and to talk over past range experiences more or less intimately. Looking back over the six weeks just behind him, Ford could not remember a single incident - a sentence, even - that had been unpleasant, unless he clung to his belief in Dick's contempt, and that he had since set down to his own super-sensitiveness. And yet -

"He's got bad eyes," he concluded. "That's what it is; I never did like eyes the color of polished steel; nickel-plated eyes, I call 'em; all shine and no color. Still, a man ain't to blame for his eyes."

Then Dick overtook him with Buddy trailing, red-eyed, at his heels, and Ford forgot, in the work to be done that day, all about his speculations. He involved himself in a fruitless argument with Buddy, upon the subject of what a seven-year-old can stand in the way of riding, and yielded finally before the quiver of Buddy's lips. They were only going over on Long Ridge, anyway, and the day was fine, and Buddy had frequently ridden as far, according to Dick. Indeed, it was Dick's easy-natured, "Ah, let the kid go, why don't you?" which gave Ford an excuse for reconsidering.

And Buddy repaid him after his usual fashion. At the supper table he looked up, round-eyed, from his plate.

"Gee, but I'm hungry!" he sighed. "I eat and eat, just like a horse eating hay, and I just can't fill up the hole in me."

"There, never mind, honey," Mrs. Kate interposed hastily, fearing worse. "Do you want more bread and butter?"

"Yes - you always use bread for stuffing, don't you? I

want to be stuffed. All the way home my b - my stomerch was a-flopping against my backbone, just like Dick's. Only Dick said -"

"Never mind what Dick said." Mrs. Kate thrust the bread toward him, half buttered.

"Dick's mad, I guess. He's mad at Ford, too."

Buddy regarded his mother gravely over the slice of bread.

"First I've heard of it," Ford remarked lightly. "I think you must be mistaken, old-timer."

But Buddy never considered himself mistaken about anything, and he did not like being told that he was, even when the pill was sweetened with the term "old-timer." He rolled his eyes at Ford resentfully.

"Dick is mad! He got mad when you galloped over where Jo's red ribbon was hanging onto a bush. I saw him a-scowling when you rolled it up and put it in your shirt pocket. Dick wanted that ribbon for his bridle; and you better give it to him. Jo ain't your girl. She's Dick's girl. And you have to tie the ribbon of your bestest girl on your bridle. That's why," he added, with belated gallantry, "I tie my own mamma's ribbons on mine. And," he returned with terrible directness to the real issue, "Jo's Dick's girl, 'cause he said so. I heard him tell Jim Felton she's his steady, all right - and you are his girl, ain't you, Jo?"

His mother had tried at first to stop him, had given up in despair, and was now sitting in a rather tragic calm, waiting for what might come of his speech.

Josephine might have saved herself some anxious moments, if she had been so minded; perhaps she would have been minded, if she had not caught Ford's eyes fixed rather intently upon her, and sensed the expectancy in them. She bit her lip, and then she laughed.

"A man shouldn't make an assertion of that sort," she said quizzically, in the direction of Buddy - though her meaning went straight across the table to another - "unless he has some reason for feeling very sure."

Buddy tried to appear quite clear as to her meaning. "Well, if you are Dick's girl, then you better make Ford give that ribbon -"

"I have plenty of ribbons, Buddy," Josephine interrupted, smiling at him still. "Don't you want one?"

"I tie my own mamma's ribbons on my bridle," Buddy rebuffed. "My mamma is my girl - you ain't. You can give your ribbons to Dick."

"Mamma won't be your girl if you don't stop talking so much at the table - and elsewhere," Mrs. Kate informed him sternly, with a glance of trepidation at the others. "A little boy mustn't talk about grown-ups, and what they do or say."

"What can I talk about, then? The boys talk about their girls all the time -"

"I wish to goodness I had let you go with your dad. I shall not let you eat with us, anyway, if you don't keep quiet. You're getting perfectly impossible." Which even Buddy understood as a protest which was not to be taken seriously.

Ford stayed long enough to finish drinking his tea, and then he left the house with what he privately considered a perfectly casual manner. As a matter of fact, he was extremely self-conscious about it, so that Mrs. Kate felt justified in mentioning it, and in asking Josephine a question or two - when she had prudently made an errand elsewhere for Buddy.

Josephine, having promptly disclaimed all knowledge or interest pertaining to the affair, Mrs. Kate spoke her mind plainly.

"If Ford's going to fall in love with you, Phenie," she said, "I think you're foolish to encourage Dick. I believe Ford is falling in love with you. I never thought he even liked you till to-night, but what Buddy said about that ribbon -"

"I don't suppose Bud knows what he's talking about - any more than you do," snapped Josephine. "If you're determined that I shall have a love affair on this ranch, I'm going home." She planted her chin in her two palms, just as she had done at dinner, and stared into vacancy.

"Where?" asked Mrs. Kate pointedly, and then atoned for it whole-heartedly. "There, I didn't mean that - only - this is your home. It's got to be; I won't let it be anywhere else. And you needn't have any love affair, Phene - you know that. Only you shan't hurt Ford. I think he's perfectly splendid! What he did for Chester - I - I can't think of that without getting a lump in my throat, Phene. Think of it! Going without food himself, because there wasn't enough for two, and - and - well, he just simply threw away his own chance of getting through, to give Chester a better one. It was the bravest thing I ever heard of! And the way he has conquered -?"

"How do you know he has conquered? Rumor says he hasn't. And lots of men save other men's lives; it's being done every day, and no one hears much about it. You think it was something extraordinary, just because it happened to be Chester that was saved. Anybody will do all he can for a sick partner, when they're away out in the wilds. I haven't a doubt Dick would have done the very same thing, when it comes to that." Josephine got up from the table then, and went haughtily into her own room.

Mrs. Kate retired quite as haughtily into the kitchen, and there was a distinct coolness between them for the rest of the day, and a part of the next. The chill of it affected Ford sufficiently to keep him away from the house as much as possible, and unusually silent and unlike himself when he was with the men.

But, unlike many another, he did not know that his recurrent dissatisfaction with life was directly traceable to the apparent intimacy between Josephine and Dick. Ford, if he had tried to put his gloomy unrest into words, would have transposed his trouble and would have mistaken effect for cause. In other words, he would have ignored Josephine and Dick entirely, and would have said that he wanted whisky - and wanted it as the damned are said to want water.

CHAPTER XII

AT HAND-GRIPS WITH THE DEMON

Mose was mad. He was flinging tinware about the kitchen with a fine disregard of the din or the dents, and whenever the blue cat ventured out from under the stove, he kicked at it viciously. He was mad at Ford; and when a man gets mad at his foreman - without knowing that the foreman has been instructed to bear with his faults and keep him on the pay-roll at any price - he must, if he be the cook, have recourse to kicking cats and banging dishes about, since he dare not kick the foreman. For in late November "jobs" are not at all plentiful in the range land, and even an angry cook must keep his job or face the world-old economic problem of food, clothing, and shelter.

But if he dared not speak his mind plainly to Ford, he was not averse to pouring his woes into the first sympathetic ear that came his way. It happened that upon this occasion the ear arrived speedily upon the head of Dick Thomas.

"Matter, Mose?" he queried, sidestepping the cat, which gave a long leap straight for the door, when it opened. "Cat been licking the butter again?"

Mose grunted and slammed three pie tins into a

B. M. Bower

cupboard with such force that two of them bounced out and rolled across the floor. One came within reach of his foot, and he kicked it into the wood-box, and swore at it while it was on the way. "And I wisht it was Ford Campbell himself, the snoopin', stingy, kitchen-grannying, booze-fightin', son-of-a-sour-dough bannock!" he finished prayerfully.

"He surely hasn't tried to mix in here, and meddle with you?" Dick asked, helping himself to a piece of pie. You know the tone; it had just that inflection of surprised sympathy which makes you tell your troubles without that reservation which a more neutral listener would unconsciously impel.

I am not going to give Mose's version, because he warped the story to make it fit his own indignation, and did not do Ford justice. This, then, is the exact truth:

Ford chanced to be walking up along the edge of the gully which ran past the bunk-house, and into which empty cans and other garbage were thrown. Sometimes a can fell short, so that all the gully edge was liberally decorated with a gay assortment of canners' labels. Just as he had come up, Mose had opened the kitchen door and thrown out a cream can, which had fallen in front of Ford and trickled a white stream upon the frozen ground. Ford had stooped and picked up the can, had shaken it, and heard the slosh which told of waste. He had investigated further, and decided that throwing out a cream can before it was quite empty was not an accident with Mose, but might be termed a habit. He had taken Exhibit A to the kitchen, but had laughed while he spoke of it. And these were his exact words:

"Lordy me, Mose! Somebody's liable to come here and

get rich off us, if we don't look out. He'll gather up the cream cans you throw into the discard and start a dairy on the leavings." Then he had set the can down on the water bench beside the door and gone away.

"I've been cookin' for cow-camps ever since I got my knee stiffened up so's't I couldn't ride - and that's sixteen year ago last Fourth - and it's the first time I ever had any darned foreman go snoopin' around my back door to see if I scrape out the cans clean!" Mose seated himself upon a corner of the table with the stiff leg for a brace and the good one swinging free, and folded his bare arms upon his heaving chest.

"And that ain't all, Dick," he went on aggrievedly. "He went and cut down the order I give him for grub. That's something Ches never done - not with me, anyway. Asked me - asked me, what I wanted with so much choc'late. And I wanted boiled cider for m' mince-meat, and never got it. And brandy, too - only I didn't put that down on the list; I knowed better than to write it out. But I give Jim money - out uh my own pocket! - to git some with, and he never done it. Said Ford told him p'tic'ler not to bring out nothin' any nearer drinkable than lemon extract! I've got a darned good mind," he added somberly, "to fire the hull works into the gully. He don't belong on no cow ranch. Where he'd oughta be is runnin' the W.C.T.U. So darned afraid of a pint uh brandy -"

"If I was dead sure your brains wouldn't get to leaking out your mouth," Dick began guardedly, "I might put you wise to something." He took a drink of water, opened the door that he might throw out what remained in the dipper, and made sure that no one was near the bunk-house before he closed the door again.

Mose watched him interestedly.

"You know me, Dick - I never do tell all I know," he hinted heavily.

"Well," Dick stood with his hand upon the door-knob and a sly grin upon his face, "I ain't saying a word about anything. Only - if you might happen to want some - eggs - for your mince pies, you might look good under the southeast corner of the third haystack, counting from the big corral. I believe there's a - nest - there."

"The deuce!" Mose brightened understandingly and drummed with his fingers upon his bare, dough-caked forearm. "Do yuh know who - er - what hen laid 'em there?"

"I do," said Dick with a rising inflection. "The head he-hen uh the flock. But if I was going to hunt eggs, I'd take down a chiny egg and leave it in the nest, Mose."

"But I ain't got -" Mose caught Dick's pale glance resting with what might be considered some significance upon the vinegar jug, and he stopped short. "That wouldn't work," he commented vaguely.

"Well, I've got to be going. Boss might can me if he caught me loafing around here, eating pie when I ought to be working. Ford's a fine fellow, don't you think?" He grinned and went out, and immediately returned, complaining that he never could stand socks with a hole in the toe, and he guessed he'd have to hunt through his war-bag for a good pair.

Mose, as need scarcely be explained, went

immediately to the stable to hunt eggs; and Dick, in the next room, smiled to himself when he heard the door slam behind him. Dick did not change his socks just then; he went first into the kitchen and busied himself there, and he continued to smile to himself. Later he went out and met Ford, who was riding moodily up from the river field.

"Say, I'm going to be an interfering kind of a cuss, and put you next to something," he began, with just the right degree of hesitation in his manner. "It ain't any of my business, but -" He stopped and lighted a cigarette. "If you'll come up to the bunk-house, I'll show you something funny!"

Ford dismounted in silence, led his horse into the stable, and without waiting to unsaddle, followed Dick.

"We've got to hurry, before Mose gets back from hunting eggs," Dick remarked, by way of explaining the long strides he took. "And of course I'm taking it for granted, Ford, that you won't say anything. I kinda thought you ought to know, maybe - but I'd never say a word if I didn't feel pretty sure you'd keep it behind your teeth."

"Well - I'm waiting to see what it is," Ford replied non-committally.

Dick opened the kitchen door, and led Ford through that into the bunk-room. "You wait here - I'm afraid Mose might come back," he said, and went into the kitchen. When he returned he had a gallon jug in his hand. He was still smiling.

"I went to mix me up some soda-water for heartburn,"

he said, "and when I picked up this jug, Mose took it out of my hand and said it was boiled cider, that he'd got for mince-meat. So when he went out, I took a taste. Here: You sample it yourself, Ford. If that's boiled cider, I wouldn't mind having a barrel!"

Ford took the jug, pulled the cork, and sniffed at the opening. He did not say anything, but he looked up at Dick significantly.

"Taste it once!" urged Dick innocently. "I'd just like to have you see the brand of slow poison a fool like Mose will pour down him."

Ford hesitated, sniffed, started to set down the jug, then lifted it and took a swallow.

"That isn't as bad as some I've seen," he pronounced evenly, shoving in the cork. "Nor as good," he added conservatively. "I wonder where he got it."

"Search me - oh, by jiminy, here he comes! I'm going to take a scoot, Ford. Don't give me away, will you? And if I was you, I wouldn't say anything to Mose - I know that old devil pretty well. He'll keep mighty quiet about it himself - unless you jump him about it. Then he'll roar around to everybody he sees, and claim it was a plant."

He slid stealthily through the outer door, and Ford saw him run down into the gully and disappear, while Mose was yet half-way from the stable.

Ford sat on the edge of a bunk and looked at the jug beside him. If Dick had deliberately planned to tempt him, he had chosen the time well; and if he had not done it deliberately, there must have been a malignant spirit abroad that day.

For twenty-four hours Ford had been more than usually restless and moody. Even Buddy had noticed that, and complained that Ford was cross and wouldn't talk to him; whereupon Mrs. Kate had scolded Josephine and accused her of being responsible for his gloom and silence. Since Josephine's conscience sustained the charge, she resented the accusation and proceeded deliberately to add to its justice; which did not make Ford any the happier, you may be sure. For when a man reaches that mental state which causes him to carry a girl's ribbon folded carefully into the most secret compartment of his pocketbook, and to avoid the girl herself and yet feel like committing assault and battery with intent to kill, because some other man occasionally rides with her for an hour or two, he is extremely sensitive to averted glances and chilly tones and monosyllabic conversation.

Since the day before, when she had ridden as far as the stage road with Dick, when he went to the line-camp, Ford had been fighting the desire to saddle a horse and ride to town; and the thing that lured him townward confronted him now in that gray stone jug with the brown neck and handle.

He lifted the jug, shook it tentatively, pulled out the cork with a jerk that was savage, and looked around the room for some place where he might empty the contents and have done with temptation; but there was no receptacle but the stove, so he started to the door with it, meaning to pour it on the ground. Mose just then shambled past the window, and Ford sat down to wait until the cook was safe in the kitchen. And all the while the cork was out of that jug, so that the fumes of the whisky rose maddeningly to his nostrils, and the little that he had swallowed whipped the thirst-devil to a fury of desire.

In the kitchen, Mose rattled pans and hummed a raucous tune under his breath, and presently he started again for the stable. Dick, desultorily bracing a leaning post of one of the corrals, saw him coming and grinned. He glanced toward the bunk-house, where Ford still lingered, and the grin grew broader. After that he went all around the corral with his hammer and bucket of nails, tightening poles and braces and, incidentally, keeping an eye upon the bunk-house; and while he worked, he whistled and smiled by turns. Dick was in an unusually cheerful mood that day.

Mose came shuffling up behind him and stood with his stiff leg thrust forward and his hands rolled up in his apron. Dick could see that he had something clasped tightly under the wrappings.

"Say, that he-hen - she laid twice in the same place!" Mose announced confidentially. "Got 'em both - for m'mince pies!" He waggled his head, winked twice with his left eye, and went back to the bunk-house.

Still Ford did not appear. Josephine came, however, in riding skirt and gray hat and gauntlets, treading lightly down the path that lay all in a yellow glow which was not so much sunlight as that mellow haze which we call Indian Summer. She looked in at the stable, and then came straight over to Dick. There was, when Josephine was her natural self, something very direct and honest about all her movements, as if she disdained all feminine subterfuges and took always the straight, open trail to her object.

"Do you know where Mr. Campbell is, Dick?" she asked him, and added no explanation of her desire to know.

"I do," said Dick, with the rising inflection which was his habit, when the words were used for a bait to catch another question.

"Well, where is he, then?"

Dick straightened up and smiled down upon her queerly. "Count ten before you ask me that again," he parried, "because maybe you'd rather not know."

Josephine lifted her chin and gave him that straight, measuring stare which had so annoyed Ford the first time he had seen her. "I have counted," she said calmly after a pause. "Where is Mr. Campbell, please?" - and the "please" pushed Dick to the very edge of her favor, it was so coldly formal.

"Well, if you're sure you counted straight, the last time I saw him he was in the bunk-house."

"Well?" The tone of her demanded more.

"He was in the bunk-house - sitting close up to a gallon jug of whisky." His eyelids flickered. "He's there yet - but I wouldn't swear to the gallon -"

"Thank you very much." This time her tone pushed him over the edge and into the depths of her disapproval. "I was sure I could depend upon you - to tell!"

"What else could I do, when you asked?"

But she had her back to him, and was walking away up the path, and if she heard, she did not trouble to answer. But in spite of her manner, Dick smiled, and brought the hammer down against a post with such force that he splintered the handle.

"Something's going to drop on this ranch, pretty quick," he prophesied, looking down at the useless tool in his hand. "And if I wanted to name it, I'd call it Ford." He glanced up the path to where Josephine was walking straight to the west door of the bunk-house, and laughed sourly. "Well, she needn't take my word for it if she don't want to, I guess," he muttered. "Nothing like heading off a critter - or a woman - in time!"

Josephine did not hesitate upon the doorstep. She opened the door and went in, and shut the door behind her before the echo of her step had died. Ford was lying as he had lain once before, upon a bunk, with his face hidden in his folded arms. He did not hear her - at any rate he did not know who it was, for he did not lift his head or stir.

Josephine looked at the jug upon the floor beside him, bent and lifted it very gently from the floor; tilted it to the window so that she could look into it, tilted her nose at the odor, and very, very gently put it back where she had found it. Then she stood and looked down at Ford with her eyebrows pinched together.

She did not move, after that, and she certainly did not speak, but her presence for all that became manifest to him. He lifted his head and stared at her over an elbow;

and his eyes were heavy with trouble, and his mouth was set in lines of bitterness.

"Did you want me for something?" he asked, when he saw that she was not going to speak first.

She shook her head. "Is it - pretty steep?" she ventured after a moment, and glanced down at the jug.

He looked puzzled at first, but when his own glance followed hers, he understood. He stared up at her somberly before he let his head drop back upon his arms, so that his face was once more hidden.

"You've never been in bell, I suppose," he told her, and his voice was dull and tired. After a minute he looked up at her impatiently. "Is it fun to stand and watch a man - What do you want, anyway? It doesn't matter - to you."

"Are you sure?" she retorted sharply. "And - suppose it doesn't. I have Kate to think of, at least."

He gave a little laugh that came nearer being a snort. "Oh, if that's all, you needn't worry. I'm not quite that far gone, thank you!"

"I was thinking of the ranch, and of her ideals, and her blind trust in you, and of the effect on the men," she explained impatiently.

He was silent a moment. "I'm thinking of myself!" he told her grimly then.

"And - don't you ever - think of me?" She set her teeth sharply together after the words were out, and watched him, breathing quickly.

Ford sprang up from the bunk and faced her with stern questioning in his eyes, but she only flushed a little under his scrutiny. Her eyes, he noticed, were clear and steady, and they had in them something of that courage which fears but will not flinch.

"I don't want to think of you!" he said, lowering his voice unconsciously. "For the last month I've tried mighty hard not to think of you. And if you want to know why - I'm married!"

She leaned back against the door and stared up at him with widening pupils. Ford looked down and struck the jug with his toe. "That thing," he said slowly, "I've got to fight alone. I don't know which is going to come out winner, me or the booze. I - don't - know." He lifted his head and looked at her. "What did you come in here for?" he asked bluntly.

She caught her breath, but she would not dodge. Ford loved her for that. "Dick told me - and I was - I wanted to - well, help. I thought I might - sometimes when the climb is too steep, a hand will keep one from - slipping."

"What made you want to help? You don't even like me." His tone was flat and unemotional, but she did not seem able to meet his eyes. So she looked down at the jug.

"Dick said - but the jug is full practically. I don't understand how -"

"It isn't as full as it ought to be; it lacks one swallow."

He eyed it queerly. "I wish I knew how much it would lack by dark," he said.

She threw out an impulsive hand. "Oh, but you must make up your mind! You mustn't temporize like that, or wonder - or -"

"This," he interrupted rather flippantly, "is something little girls can't understand. They'd better not try. This isn't a woman's problem, to be solved by argument. It's a man's fight!"

"But if you would just make up your mind, you could win."

"Could I?" His tone was amusedly skeptical, but his eyes were still somber.

"Even a woman," she said impatiently, "knows that is not the way to win a fight - to send for the enemy and give him all your weapons, and a plan of the fortifications, and the password; when you know there's no mercy to be hoped for!"

He smiled at her simile, and at her earnestness also, perhaps; but that black gloom remained, looking out of his eyes.

"What made you send for it? A whole gallon!"

"I didn't send for it. That jug belongs to Mose," he told her simply. "Dick told me Mose had it; rather, Dick went into the kitchen and got it, and turned it over to me." In spite of the words, he did not give one the impression that he was defending himself; he was merely offering an explanation because she seemed to demand one.

"Dick got it and turned it over to you!" Her forehead wrinkled again into vertical lines. She studied him frowningly. "Will you give it to me?" she asked directly.

Ford folded his arms and scowled down at the jug. "No," he refused at last, "I won't. If booze is going to be the boss of me I want to know it. And I can't know it too quick."

"But - you're only human, Ford!"

"Sure. But I'm kinda hoping I'm a man, too." His eyes lightened a little while they rested upon her.

"But you've got the poison of it - it's like a traitor in your fort, ready to open the door. You can't do it! I - oh, you'll never understand why, but I can't let you risk it. You've got to let me help; give it to me, Ford!"

"No, You go on to the house, and don't bother about me. You can't help - nobody can. It's up to me."

She struck her hands together in a nervous rage. "You want to keep it because you want to drink it! If you didn't want it, you'd hate to be near it. You'd want some one to take it away. You just want to get drunk, and be a beast. You - you - oh - you don't know what you're doing, or how much it means! You don't know!" Her hands went up suddenly and covered her face.

Ford walked the length of the room away from her, turned and came back until he faced her where she stood leaning against the door, with her face still hidden behind her palms. He reached out his arms to her, hesitated, and drew them back.

"I wish you'd go," he said. "There are some things harder to fight than whisky. You only make it worse."

"I'll go when you give me that." She flung a hand out toward the jug.

"You'll go anyway!" He took her by the arm, quietly pulled her away from the door, opened it, and then closed it while, for just a breath or two, he held her tightly clasped in his arms. Very gently, after that, he pushed her out upon the doorstep and shut the door behind her. The lock clicked a hint which she could not fail to hear and understand. He waited until he heard her walk away, sat down with the air of a man who is very, very weary, rested his elbows upon his knees, and with his hands clasped loosely together, he glowered at the jug on the floor. Then the soul of Ford Campbell went deep down into the pit where all the devils dwell.

CHAPTER XIII

A PLAN GONE WRONG

It was Mose crashing headlong into the old messbox where he kept rattly basins, empty lard pails, and such, that roused Ford. He got up and went into the kitchen, and when he saw what was, the matter, extricated Mose by the simple method of grabbing his shoulders and pulling hard; then he set the cook upon his feet, and got full in his face the unmistakable fumes of whisky.

"What? You got another jug?" he asked, with some disgust, steadying Mose against the wall.

"Ah - I ain't got any jug uh nothin'," Mose protested, rather thickly. "And I never took them bottles outa the stack; that musta bcen Dick done that. Get after him about it; he's the one told me where yuh hid 'em - but I never touched 'em, honest I never. If they're gone, you get after Dick. Don't yuh go 'n' lay it on me, now!" He was whimpering with maudlin pathos before he finished. Ford scowled at him thoughtfully.

"Dick told you about the bottles in the haystack, did he?" he asked. "Which stack was it? And how many bottles?"

Mose gave him a bleary stare. "Aw, you know. You hid 'em there yourself! Dick said so. I ain't goin' to say which stack, or how many bottles - or - any other - darn thing about it." He punctuated his phrases by prodding a finger against Ford's chest, and he wagged his head with all the self-consciousness of spurious virtue. "Promised Dick I wouldn't, and I won't. Not a - darn - word about it. Wanted some - for m' mince-meat, but I never took any outa the haystack." Whereupon he began to show a pronounced limpness in his good leg, and a tendency to slide down upon the floor.

Ford piloted him to a chair, eased him into it, and stood over him in frowning meditation. Mose was drunk; absolutely, undeniably drunk. It could not have been the jug, for the jug was full. Till then the oddity of a full jug of whisky in Mose's kitchen after at least twenty-four hours must have elapsed since its arrival, had not occurred to him. He had been too preoccupied with his own fight to think much about Mose.

"Shay, I never took them bottles outa the stack," Mose looked up to protest solemnly. "Dick never told me about 'em, neither. Dick tol' me -" tapping Ford's arm with his finger for every word, " - 'at there was aigs down there, for m' mince-meat." He stopped suddenly and goggled up at Ford. "Shay, yuh don't put aigs in - mince-meat," he informed him earnestly. "Not a darn aig! That's what Dick tol' me - aigs for m' mince-meat. Oh, I knowed right off what he meant, all right," he explained proudly. "He didn't wanta come right out 'n' shay what it was - an' I - got - the - aigs!"

"Yes - how many - eggs?" Ford held himself rigidly quiet.

B. M. Bower

"Two quart - aigs!" Mose laughed at the joke. "I wisht," he added pensively, "the hens'd all lay them kinda aigs. I'd buy up all the shickens in - the whole worl'." He gazed raptly upon the vision the words conjured. "Gee! Quart aigs - 'n' all the shickens in the worl' layin' reg'lar!"

"Have you got any left?"

"No - honest. Used 'em all up - for m' mince-meat!"

Ford knew he was lying. His eyes searched the untidy tables and the corners filled with bags and boxes. Mose was a good cook, but his ideas of order were vague, and his system of housekeeping was the simple one of leaving everything where he had last been using it, so that it might be handy when he wanted it again. A dozen bottles might be concealed there, like the faces in a picture-puzzle, and it would take a housecleaning to disclose them all. But Ford, when he knew that no bottle had been left in sight, began turning over the bags and looking behind the boxes.

He must have been "growing warm" when he stood wondering whether it was worth while to look into the flour-bin, for Mose gave an inarticulate snarl and pounced on him from behind. The weight of him sent Ford down on all fours and kept him there for a space, and even after he was up he found himself quite busy. Mose was a husky individual, with no infirmity of the arms and fists, even if he did have a stiff leg, and drunkenness frequently flares and fades in a man like a candle guttering in the wind. Besides, Mose was fighting to save his whisky.

Still, Ford had not sent all of Sunset into its cellars,

figuratively speaking, for nothing; and while a man may feel more enthusiasm for fighting when under the influence of the stuff that cheers sometimes and never fails to inebriate, the added incentive does not necessarily mean also added muscular development or more weight behind the punch. Ford, fighting as he had always fought, be he drunk or sober, came speedily to the point where he could inspect a skinned knuckle and afterwards gaze in peace upon his antagonist.

He was occupied with both diversions when the door was pushed open as by a man in great haste. He looked up from the knuckle into the expectant eyes of Jim Felton, and over the shoulder of Jim he saw a gloating certainty writ large upon the face of Dick Thomas. They had been running; he could tell that by their uneven breathing, and it occurred to him that they must have heard the clamor when he pitched Mose head first into the dish cupboard. There had been considerable noise about that time, he remembered; they must also have heard the howl Mose gave at the instant of contact. Ford glanced involuntarily at that side of the room where stood the cupboard, and mentally admitted that it looked like there had been a slight disagreement, or else a severe seismic disturbance; and Montana is not what one calls an earthquake country. His eyes left the generous sprinkle of broken dishes on the floor, with Mose sprawled inertly in their midst, looking not unlike a broken platter himself - or one badly nicked - and rested again upon the grinning face behind the shoulder of Jim Felton.

Ford was ever a man of not many words, even when he had a grievance. He made straight for Dick, and when he had pushed Jim out of the way, he reached him violently. Dick tottered upon the step and went off backward, and Ford landed upon him fairly and with full knowledge and intent.

Jim Felton was a wise young man. He stood back and let them fight it out, and when it was over he said never a word until Dick had picked himself up and walked off, holding to his nose a handkerchief that reddened rapidly.

"Say, you are a son-of-a-gun to fight," he observed admiringly then to Ford. "Don't you know Dick's supposed to be abso-lute-ly unlickable?"

"May be so - but he sure shows all the symptoms of being licked right at present." Ford moved a thumb joint gently to see whether it was really dislocated or merely felt that way.

"He's going up to the house now, to tell the missus," remarked Jim, craning his neck from the doorway.

"If he does that," Ford replied calmly, "I'll half kill him next time. What I gave him just now is only a sample package left on the doorstep to try." He sat down upon a corner of the table and began to make himself a smoke. "Is he going up to the house - honest?" He would not yield to the impulse to look and see for himself.

"We-el, the trail he's taking has no other logical destination," drawled Jim. "He's across the bridge." When Ford showed no disposition to say anything to that, Jim came in and closed the door. "Say, what laid old Mose out so nice?" he asked, with an indolent sort of curiosity. "Booze? Or just bumps?"

"A little of both," said Ford indifferently, between puffs. He was thinking of the tale Dick would tell at the house, and he was thinking of the probable effect upon one listener; the other didn't worry him, though he liked Mrs. Kate very much.

Jim went over and investigated; discovering that Mose was close to snoring, he sat upon a corner of the other table, swung a spurred boot, and regarded Ford interestedly over his own cigarette building. "Say, for a man that's supposed to be soused," he began, after a silence, "you act and talk remarkably lucid. I wish I could carry booze like that," he added regretfully. "But I can't; my tongue and my legs always betray the guilty secret. Have you got any particular system, or is it just a gift?"

"No" - Ford shook his head - "nothing like that. I just don't happen to be drunk." He eyed Jim sharply while he considered within himself. "It looks to me," he began, after a moment, "as if our friend Dick had framed up a nice little plant. One way and another I got wise to the whole thing; but for the life of me, I can't see what made him do it. Lordy me! I never kicked him on any bunion!" He grinned, as memory flashed a brief, mental picture of Sunset and certain incidents which occurred there. But memory never lets well enough alone, and one is lucky to escape without seeing a picture that leaves a sting; Ford's smile ended in a scowl.

"Jealousy, old man," Jim pronounced without hesitation. "Of course, I don't know the details, but - details be darned. If he has tried to hand you a package, take it from me, jealousy's the string he tied it with. I don't mind saying that Dick told me when I first rode up to the corral that you and Mose were both boozing up to beat the band; and right after that we heard a deuce of a racket up here, and it did look -" He waved an apologetic hand at Mose and the fragments of pottery which framed like a "still life" picture on the floor, and let it go at that. "I'm strong for you, Ford," he added, and his smile was frank and friendly. "Double Cross is the name of this outfit, but I'm all in favor of running that brand on the cow-critters and keeping it out of the bunk-house. If you should happen to feel like elucidating -" he hinted delicately.

Ford had always liked Jim Felton; now he warmed to him as a real friend, and certain things he told him. As much about the jug with the brown neck and handle as concerned Dick, and all he knew of the bottles in the haystack, while Jim smoked, and swung the foot which did not rest upon the floor, and listened.

"Sounds like Dick, all right," he passed judgment, when Ford had finished. "He counted on your falling for the jug - and oh, my! It was a beautiful plant. I'd sure hate to have anybody sing 'Yield not to temptation' at me, if a gallon jug of the real stuff fell into my arms and nobody was looking." He eyed Ford queerly. "You've got quite a reputation - " he ventured.

"Well, I earned it," Ford observed laconically.

"Dick banked on it - I'd stake my whole stack of blues on that. And after you'd torn up the ranch, and pitched the fragments into the gulch, he'd hold the last trump, with all high cards to keep the lead. Whee!" He meditated admiringly upon the strategy. "But what I can't seem to understand," he said frankly, "is why the deuce it didn't work! Is your swallower out of kilter? If you don't mind my asking!"

"I never noticed that it was paralyzed," Ford answered grimly. He got up, lifted a lid of the stove, and threw in the cigarette stub mechanically. Then he bethought him of his interrupted search, and prodded a long-handled spoon into the flour bin, struck something smooth and hard, and drew out a befloured, quart bottle half full of whisky. He wiped the bottle carefully, inspected it briefly, and pitched it into the gully, where it smashed odorously upon a rock. Jim, watching him, knew that he was thinking all the while of something else. When Ford spoke, he proved it.

"Are you any good at all in the kitchen, Jim?" he asked, turning to him as if he had decided just how he would meet the situation.

"Well, I hate to brag, but I've known of men eating my grub and going right on living as if nothing had happened," Jim admitted modestly.

"Well, you turn yourself loose in here, will you? The boys will be good and empty when they come - it's dinner time right now. I'll help you carry Mose out of the way before I go."

Jim looked as if he would like to ask what Ford meant to do, but he refrained. There was something besides preoccupation in Ford's face, and it did not make for easy questioning. Jim did yield to his curiosity to the extent of watching through a window, when Ford went out, to see where he was going; and when he saw Ford had the jug, and that he took the path which led across the little bridge and so to the house, he drew back and said "Whee-e-e!" under his breath. Then he remarked to the recumbent Mose, who was not in a condition either to hear or understand: "I'll bet you Dick's got all he wants, right now, without any postscript." After which Jim hunted up a clean apron and proceeded, with his spurs on his heels, his hat on the back of his head, and a smile upon his lips, to sweep out the broken dishes so that he might walk without hearing them crunch unpleasantly under his boots. "I'll take wildcats in mine, please," he remarked once irrelevantly aloud, and smiled again.

CHAPTER XIV

THE FEMININE POINT OF VIEW

When Ford stepped upon the porch with the jug in his hand, he gave every indication of having definitely made up his mind. When he glimpsed Josephine's worried face behind the lace curtain in the window, he dropped the jug lower and held it against his leg in such a way as to indicate that he hoped she could not see it, but otherwise he gave no sign of perturbation. He walked along the porch to the door of his own room, went in, locked the door after him, and put the jug down on a chair. He could hear faint sounds of dishes being placed upon the table in the dining-room, which was next to his own, and he knew that dinner was half an hour late; which was unusual in Mrs. Kate's orderly domain. Mrs. Kate was one of those excellent women whose house is always immaculate, whose meals are ever placed before one when the clock points to a certain hour, and whose table never lacks a salad and a dessert - though how those feats are accomplished upon a cattle ranch must ever remain a mystery. Ford was therefore justified in taking the second look at his watch and in holding it up to his ear, and also in lifting his eyebrows when all was done. Fifteen minutes by the watch it was before he heard the silvery tinkle of the tea bell, which was one of the ties which bound Mrs. Kate to civilization, and which

B. M. Bower

announced that he might enter the dining-room.

He went in as clean and fresh and straight-backed and quiet as ever he had done, and when he saw that the room was empty save for Buddy, perched upon his long-legged chair with his heels hooked over the top round and a napkin tucked expectantly inside the collar of his blue blouse, he took in the situation and sat down without waiting for the women. The very first glance told him that Mrs. Kate had never prepared that meal. It was, putting it bluntly, a scrappy affair hastily gathered from various shelves in the pantry and hurriedly arranged haphazard upon the table.

Buddy gazed upon the sprinkle of dishes with undisguised dissatisfaction. "There ain't any potatoes," he announced gloomily. "My own mamma always cooks potatoes. Josephine's the limit! I been working to-day. I almost dug out a badger, over by the bluff. I got where I could hear him scratching to get away, and then it was all rocks, so I couldn't dig any more. Gee, it was hard digging! And I'm just about starved, if you want to know. And there ain't any potatoes."

"Bread and butter is fine when you're hungry," Ford suggested, and spread a slice for Buddy, somewhat inattentively, because he was also keeping an eye upon the kitchen door, where he had caught a fleeting glimpse of Josephine looking in at him.

"You're putting the butter all in one place," Buddy criticised, with his usual frankness. "I guess you're drunk, all right. If you're too drunk to spread butter, let me do it."

"What makes you think I'm drunk?" Ford questioned,

lowering his voice because of the person he suspected was in the kitchen.

"Mamma and Jo was quarreling about it; that's why. And my own mamma cried, and shut the door, and wouldn't let me go in. And Jo pretty near cried too, all right. I guess she did, only not when any one was looking. Her eyes are awful red, anyway." Buddy took great, ravenous bites of the bread and butter and eyed Ford unwinkingly.

"What's disslepointed?" he demanded abruptly, after he had given himself a white mustache with his glass of milk.

"Why do you want to know?"

"That's what my own mamma is, and that's what Jo is. Only my own mamma is it about you, and Jo's it about mamma. Say, did you lick Dick? Jo told my own mamma she wisht you'd killed him. Jo's awful mad to-day. I guess she's mad at Dick, because he ain't very much of a fighter. Did you lick him easy? Did you paste him one in the jaw?"

Josephine entered then with Ford's belated tea. Her eyelids were pink, as Buddy had told him, and she did not look at him while she filled his cup.

"Kate has a sick headache," she explained primly, "and I did the best I could with lunch. I hope it's -"

"It is," Ford interrupted reassuringly. "Everything is fine and dandy."

"You didn't cook any potatoes!" Buddy charged

mercilessly. "And Ford's too drunk to put the butter on right. I'm going to tell my dad that next time he goes to Oregon I'm going along. This outfit will sure go to the devil if he stays much longer!"

"Where did you hear that, Bud?" Josephine asked, still carefully avoiding a glance at Ford.

"Well, Dick said it would go to the devil. I guess," he added on his own account, with an eloquent look at the table, "it's on the trail right now."

Ford looked at Josephine, opened his lips to say that it might still be headed off, and decided not to speak. There was a stubborn streak in Ford Campbell. She had said some bitter things, in her anger. Perhaps she had not entirely believed them herself, and perhaps Mrs. Kate had not been accurately quoted by her precocious young son; she may not have said that she was disappointed in Ford. They might not have believed whatever it was Dick told them, and they might still have full confidence in him, Ford Campbell. Still, there was the stubborn streak which would not explain or defend. So he left the table, and went into his own room without any word save a muttered excuse; and that in spite of the fact that Josephine looked full at him, at last, and with a wistfulness that moved him almost to the point of taking her in his arms and kissing away the worry - if he could.

He went up to the table where stood the jug, looked at it, lifted it, and set it down again. Then he lifted it again and pulled the cork out with a jerk, wondering if the sound of it had reached through the thin partition to the ears of Josephine; he was guilty of hoping so. He put back the cork - this time carefully - walked to the outer door, turned the key, opened the door, and closed it again with a slam. Then, with a grim set of the lips, he walked softly into the closet and pulled the door nearly shut.

He knew there was a chance that Josephine, if she were interested in his movements, would go immediately into the sitting-room, where she could see the path, and would know that he had not really left the house. But she did not, evidently. She sat long enough in the dining-room for Ford to call himself a name or two and to feel exceedingly foolish over the trick, and to decide that it was a very childish one for a grown man to play upon a woman. Then she pushed back her chair, came straight toward his room, opened the door, and looked in; Ford knew, for he saw her through the crack he had left in the closet doorway. She stood there looking at the jug on the table, then went up and lifted it, much as Ford had done, and pulled the cork with a certain angry defiance. Perhaps, he guessed shrewdly, Josephine also felt rather foolish at what she was doing - and he smiled over the thought.

Josephine turned the jug to the light, shut one eye into an adorable squint, and peered in. Then she set the jug down and pushed the cork slowly into place; and her face was puzzled. Ford could have laughed aloud when he saw it, but instead he held his breath for fear she should discover him. She stood very still for a minute or two, staring at nothing at all; moved the jug into the exact place where it had stood before, and went out of the room on her toes.

So did Ford, for that matter, and he was in a cold terror lest she should look out and see him walking down the path where he should logically have walked more than five minutes before. He did not dare to turn and look - until he was outside the gate; then inspiration came to aid him and he went back boldly, stepped upon the porch with no effort at silence, opened his door, and went in as one who has a right there.

He heard the click of dishes which told that she was clearing the table, and he breathed freer. He walked across the room, waited a space, and walked back again, and then went out with his heart in its proper position in his chest; Ford was unused to feeling his heart rise to his palate, and the sensation was more novel than agreeable. When he went again down the path, there was a certain exhilaration in his step. His thoughts arranged themselves in clear-cut sentences, as if he were speaking, instead of those vague, almost wordless impressions which fill the brain ordinarily.

"She's keeping cases on that jug. She must care, or she wouldn't do that. She's worried a whole lot; I could see that, all along. Down at the bunk-house she called me Ford twice - and she said it meant a lot to her, whether I make good or not. I wonder - Lordy me! A man could make good, all right, and do it easy, if she cared! She doesn't know what to think - that jug staying right up to high-water mark, like that!" He laughed then, silently, and dwelt upon the picture she had made while she had stood there before the table.

"Lord! she'd want to kill me if she knew I hid in that closet, but I just had a hunch - that is, if she cared anything about it. I wonder if she did really say she wished I'd killed Dick?

"Anyway, I can fight it now, with her keeping cases on the quiet. I know I can fight it. Lordy me, I've got to fight it! I've got to make good; that's all there is about it. Wonder what she'll think when she sees that jug don't go down any? Wonder - oh, hell! She'd never care anything about me. If she did -" His thoughts went hazy with vague speculation, then clarified suddenly into one hard fact, like a rock thrusting up through the lazy sweep of a windless tide. "If she did care, I couldn't do anything. I'm married!"

His step lost a little of its spring, then, and he went into the bunk-house with much the same expression on his face as when he had left it an hour or so before.

He did not see Dick that day. The other boys watched him covertly, it seemed to him, and showed a disposition to talk among themselves. Jim was whistling cheerfully in the kitchen. He turned his head and laughed when Ford went in.

"I found a dead soldier behind the sack of spuds," Jim announced, and produced an empty bottle, mate to the one Ford had thrown into the gully. "And Dick didn't seem to have any appetite at all, and Mose is still in Sleepytown. I guess that's all the news at this end of the line. Er - hope everything is all right at the house?"

"Far as I could see, it was," Ford replied, with an inner sense of evasion. "I guess we'll just let her go as she looks, Jim. Did you say anything to the boys?"

Jim reddened under his tan, but he laughed disarmingly. "I cannot tell a lie," he confessed honestly, "and it was too good to keep to myself. I'm the most generous fellow you ever saw, when it comes to passing along a good story that won't hurt anybody's digestion. You don't care, do you? The joke ain't on you."

"If you'd asked me about it, I'd have said keep it under your hat. But -"

"And that would have been a sin and a shame," argued Jim, licking a finger he had just scorched on a hot kettle-handle. "The fellows all like a good story - and it don't sound any worse because it's on Dick. And say! I kinda got a clue to where he connected with that whisky. Walt says he come back from the line-camp with his overcoat rolled up and tied behind the saddle - and it wasn't what you could call a hot night, either. He musta had that jug wrapped up in it. I'll bet he sent in by Peterson, the other day, for it. He was over there, I know. He's sure a deliberate kind of a cuss, isn't he? Must have had this thing all figured out a week ago. The boys are all tickled to death at the way he got it in the neck; they know Dick pretty well. But if you'd told me not to say anything, I'd have said he stubbed his toe on his shadow and fell all over himself, and let it go at that."

"Lordy me! Jim, you needn't worry about it; you ought to know you can't keep a thing like this quiet, on a ranch. It doesn't matter much how he got that whisky here, either; I know well enough you didn't haul it out. I'd figured it out about as Walt says.

"Say, it looks as if you'll have to wrastle with the pots and pans till to-morrow. The lower fence I'll ride, this afternoon; did you get clear around the Pinnacle field?"

"I sure did - and she's tight as a drum. Say, Mose is a good cook, but he's a mighty punk housekeeper, if you ask me. I'm thinking of getting to work here with a hoe!"

So life, which had of late loomed big and bitter before the soul of Ford, slipped back into the groove of daily routine.

B. M. Bower

CHAPTER XV

THE CLIMB

Into its groove of routine slipped life at the Double Cross, but it did not move quite as smoothly as before. It was as if the "hill" which Ford was climbing suffered small landslides here and there, which threatened to block the trail below. Sometimes - still keeping to the simile - it was but a pebble or two kicked loose by Ford's heel; sometimes a bowlder which one must dodge.

Dick, for instance, must have likened Mose to a real landslide when he came at him the next day, with a roar of rage and the rolling-pin. Mose had sobered to the point where he wondered how it had all happened, and wanted to get his hands in the wool of the "nigger" said to lurk in woodpiles. He asked Jim, with various embellishments of speech, what it was all about, and Jim told him and told him truly.

"He was trying to queer you with the outfit, Mose, and that's a fact," he finished; which was the only exaggeration Jim was guilty of, for Dick had probably thought very little of Mose and his ultimate standing with the Double Cross. "And he was trying to queer Ford - but you can search me for the reason why he didn't make good, there."

Mose, like many of us, was a self-centered individual. He wasted a minute, perhaps, thinking of the trick upon Ford; but he spent all of that forenoon and well into the afternoon in deep meditation upon the affair as it concerned himself. And the first time Dick entered the presence of the cook, he got the result of Mose's reasoning.

"Tried to git me in bad, did yuh? Thought you'd git me fired, hey?" he shouted, as a sort of punctuation to the belaboring.

A rolling pin is considered a more or less fearsome weapon in the hands of a woman, I believe; when wielded by an incensed man who stands close to six feet and weighs a solid two hundred pounds, and who has the headache which follows inevitably in the wake of three pints of whisky administered internally in the short space of three hours or so, a rolling-pin should justly be classed with deadly weapons.

Jim said afterward that he never had believed it possible to act out the rough stuff of the silly supplements in the Sunday papers, but after seeing Mose perform with that rolling-pin, he was willing to call every edition of the "funny papers" realistic to a degree. Since it was Jim who helped pull Mose off, naturally he felt qualified to judge. Jim told Ford about the affair with sober face and eyes that laughed.

"And where's Dick?" Ford asked him, without committing himself upon the justice of the chastisement.

"Gone to bed, I believe. He didn't come out with anything worse than bumps, I guess - but what I saw of them are sure peaches; or maybe Italian prunes would hit them off closer; they're a fine purple shade. I ladled Three H all over him."

"I thought Dick was a fighter from Fighterville," grinned Ford, trying hard to remain non-committal and making a poor job of it.

"Well, he is, when he can stand up and box according to rule, or hit a man when he isn't looking. But my, oh! This wasn't a fight, Ford; this was like the pictures you see of an old woman lambasting her son-in-law with an umbrella. Dick never got a chance to begin. Whee-ee! Mose sure can handle a rolling-pin some!"

Ford laughed and went up to the house to his supper, and to the constrained atmosphere which was telling on his nerves more severely than did the gallon jug in his closet, and the moral effort it cost to keep that jug full to the neck.

He went in quietly, threw his hat on the bed, and sat down with an air of discouragement. It was not yet six o'clock, and he knew that Mrs. Kate would not have supper ready; but he wanted a quiet place in which to think, and he was closer to Josephine; though he would never have admitted to himself that her nearness was any comfort to him. He did admit, however, that the jug with the brown neck and handle pulled him to the room many times in spite of himself. He would take it from the corner of the closet and let his fingers close over the cork, but so far he had never yielded beyond that point. Always he had been able to set the jug back unopened.

He was getting circles under his eyes, two new creases had appeared on each side of his whimsical lips, and a permanent line was forming between his eyebrows; but he had not opened the jug, and it had been in his possession thirty-six hours. Thirty-six hours is not long, to be sure, when life runs smoothly with slight incidents to emphasize the figures on the dial, but it may seem long to the poor devil on the rack.

Just now Ford was trying to forget that a gallon of whisky stood in the right-hand corner of his closet, behind a pair of half-worn riding-boots that pinched his instep so that he seldom wore them, and that he had only to take the jug out from behind the boots, pull the cork, and lift the jug to his lips -

He caught himself leaning forward and staring at the closet door until his eyes ached with the strain. He drew back and passed his hand over his forehead; it ached, and he wanted to think about what he ought to do with Dick. He did not like to discharge him without first consulting Mrs. Kate, for he knew that Ches Mason was in the habit of talking things over with her, and since Mason was gone, she had assumed an air of latent authority. But Mrs. Kate had looked at him with such reproachful eyes, that day at dinner, and her voice had sounded so squeezed and unnatural, that he had felt too far removed from her for any discussion whatever to take place between them.

Besides, he knew he could prove absolutely nothing against Dick, if Dick were disposed toward flat denial. He might suspect - but the facts showed Ford the aggressor, and Mose also. What if Mrs. Kate declined to believe that Dick had put that jug of whisky in the kitchen, and had afterward given it to Ford? Ford had no means of knowing just what tale Dick had told her, but he did know that Mrs. Kate eyed him doubtfully, and that her conversation was forced and her manner constrained.

And Josephine was worse. Josephine had not spoken to him all that day. At breakfast she had not been present, and at dinner she had kept her eyes upon her plate and had nothing to say to any one.

He wished Mason was home, so that he could leave. It wouldn't matter then, he tried to believe, what he did. He even dwelt upon the desire of Mason's return to the extent of calculating, with his eyes upon the fancy calendar on the wall opposite, the exact time of his absence. Ten days - there was no hope of release for another month, at least, and Ford sighed unconsciously when he thought of it; for although a month is not long, there was Josephine refusing to look at him, and there was Dick - and there was the jug in the closet.

As to Josephine, there was no help for it; he could not avoid her without making the avoidance plain to all observers, and Ford was proud. As to Dick, he would not send him off without some proof that he had broken an unwritten law of the Double Cross and brought whisky to the ranch; and of that he had no proof. As to his suspicions - well, he considered that Dick had almost paid the penalty for having roused them, and the matter would have to rest where it was; for Ford was just. As to the jug, he could empty it upon the ground and be done with that particular form of torture. But he felt sure that Josephine was secretly "keeping cases" on the jug; and Ford was stubborn.

That night Ford did not respond to the tinkle of the tea bell. His head ached abominably, and he did not want to see Josephine's averted face opposite him at the table. He lay still upon the bed where he had finally thrown himself, and let the bell tinkle until it was tired.

They sent Buddy in to see why he did not come. Buddy looked at him with the round, curious eyes of precocious childhood and went back and reported that Ford wasn't asleep, but was just lying there mad. Ford heard the shrill little voice innocently maligning him, and swore to himself; but, he did not move for all that. He lay thinking and fighting discouragement and thirst, while little table sounds came through the partition and made a clicking accompaniment to his thoughts.

If he were free, he was wondering between spells of temptation, would it do any good? Would Josephine care? There was no answer to that, or if there was he did not know what it was.

After awhile the two women began talking; he judged that Buddy had left them, because it was sheer madness to speak so freely before him. At first he paid no attention to what they were saying, beyond a grudging joy in the sound of Josephine's voice. It had come to that, with Ford! But when he heard his name spoken, and by her, he lifted shamelessly to an elbow and listened, glad that the walls were so thin, and that those who dwell in thin-partitioned houses are prone to forget that the other rooms may not be quite empty. They two spent most of their waking hours alone together, and habit breeds carelessness always.

"Do you suppose he's drunk?" Mrs. Kate asked, and her voice was full of uneasiness. "Chester says he's terrible when he gets started. I was sure he was perfectly safe! I just can't stand it to have him like this. Dick told me he's drinking a little all the time, and there's no telling when he'll break out, and - Oh, I think it's perfectly terrible!"

"Hsh-sh," warned Josephine.

"He went out, quite a while ago. I heard him," said Mrs. Kate, with rash certainty. "He hasn't been like himself since that day he fought Dick. He must be -"

"But how could he?" Josephine's voice interrupted sharply. "That jug he's got is full yet."

Ford could imagine Mrs. Kate shaking her head with the wisdom born of matrimony.

"Don't you suppose he could keep putting in water?" she asked pityingly. Ford almost choked when he heard that!

"I don't believe he would." Josephine's tone was dubious. "It doesn't seem to me that a man would do that; he'd think he was just spoiling what was left. That," she declared with a flash of inspiration, "is what a woman would do. And a man always does something different!" There was a pathetic note in the last sentence, which struck Ford oddly.

"Don't think you know men, my dear, until you've been married to one for eight years or so," said Mrs. Kate patronizingly. "When you've been -"

"Oh, for mercy's sake, do you think they're all alike?" Josephine's voice was tart and impatient. "I know enough about men to know they're all different. You can't judge one by another. And I don't believe that Ford is drinking at all. He's just -"

"Just what? - since you know so well!" Mrs. Kate was growing ironical.

"He's trying not to - and worrying." Her voice lowered until it took love to hear it. Ford did hear, and his breath came fast. He did not catch Mrs. Kate's reply; he was not in love with Mrs. Kate, and he was engaged in letting the words of Josephine sink into his very soul, and in telling himself over and over that she understood. It seemed to him a miracle of intuition, that she should sense the fight he was making; and since he felt that way about it, it was just as well he did not know that Jim Felton sensed it quite as keenly as Josephine - and with a far greater understanding of how bitter a fight it was, and for that reason a deeper sympathy.

"I wish Chester was here!" wailed Mrs. Kate, across the glow of his exultant thoughts. "I'm afraid to say anything to him myself, he's so morose. It's a shame, because he's so splendid when he's - himself."

"He's as much himself now as ever he was," Josephine defended hotly. "When he's drinking he's altogether -"

"You never saw him drunk," Mrs. Kate pointed to the weak spot in Josephine's defense of him. "Dick says -"

"Oh, do you believe everything Dick says? A week ago you were bitter against Dick and all enthusiasm for Ford."

"You were flirting with Dick then, and you'd hardly treat Ford decently. And Ford hadn't gone to drink -"

"Will you hush?" There were tears of anger in

B. M. Bower

Josephine's voice. "He isn't, I tell you!"

"What does he keep that jug in the closet for? And every few hours he comes up to the house and goes into his room - and he never did that before. And have you noticed his eyes? He'll scarcely talk any more, and he just pretends to eat. At dinner to-day he scarcely touched a thing! It's a sure sign, Phenie."

Ford was growing tired of that sort of thing. It dimmed the radiance of Josephine's belief in him, to have Mrs. Kate so sure of his weakness. He got up from the bed as quietly as he could and left the house. He was even more thoughtful, after that, but not quite so gloomy - if one cared enough for his moods to make a fine distinction.

Have you ever observed the fact that many of life's grimmest battles and deepest tragedies scarce ripple the surface of trivial things? We are always rubbing elbows with the big issues and never knowing anything about it. Certainly no one at the Double Cross guessed what was always in the mind of the foreman. Jim thought he was "sore" because of Dick. Dick thought Ford was jealous of him, and trying to think of some scheme to "play even," without coming to open war. Mrs. Kate was positive, in her purely feminine mind - which was a very good mind, understand, but somewhat inadequate when brought to bear upon the big problems of life - that Ford was tippling in secret. Josephine thought - just what she said, probably, upon the chill day when she calmly asked Ford at the breakfast table if he would let her go with him.

Ford had casually remarked, in answer to a diffident question from Mrs. Kate, that he was going to ride out on Long Ridge and see if any stock was drifting back toward the ranch. He hadn't sent any one over that way for several days. Ford, be it said, had announced his intention deliberately, moved by a vague, unreasoning impulse.

"Can I go?" teased Buddy, from sheer force of habit; no one ever mentioned going anywhere, but Buddy shot that question into the conversation.

"No, you can't. You can't, with that cold," his mother vetoed promptly, and Buddy, whimpering over his hot cakes, knew well the futility of argument, when Mrs. Kate used that tone of finality.

"Will you let me go?" Josephine asked unexpectedly, and looked straight at Ford. But though her glance was direct, it was unreadable, and Ford mentally threw up his hands after one good look at her, and tried not to betray the fact that this was what he had wanted, but had not hoped for.

"Sure, you can go," he said, with deceitful brevity. Josephine had not spoken to him all the day before, except to say good-morning when he came in to his breakfast. Ford made no attempt to understand her, any more. He was carefully giving her the lead, as he would have explained it, and was merely following suit until he got a chance to trump; but he was beginning to have a discouraged feeling that the game was hers, and that he might as well lay down his hand and be done with it. Which, when he brought the simile back to practical affairs, meant that he was thinking seriously of leaving the ranch and the country just as soon as Mason returned.

He was thinking of trying the Argentine Republic for awhile, if he could sell the land which he had rashly bought while he was getting rid of his inheritance.

She did not offer any excuse for the request, as most women would have done. Neither did she thank him, with lips or with eyes, for his ready consent. She seemed distrait - preoccupied, as if she, also, were considering some weighty question.

Ford pushed back his chair, watching her furtively. She rose with Kate, and glanced toward the window.

"I suppose I shall need my heaviest sweater," she remarked practically, and as if the whole affair were too commonplace for discussion. "It does look threatening. How soon will you want to start?" This without looking toward Ford at all.

"Right away, if that suits you." Ford was still watchful, as if he had not quite given up hope of reading her meaning.

She told him she would be ready by the time he had saddled, and she appeared in the stable door while he was cinching the saddle on the horse he meant to ride.

"I hope you haven't given me Dude," she said unemotionally. "He's supposed to be gentle - but he bucked me off that day I sprained my ankle, and all the excuse he had was that a rabbit jumped out from a bush almost under his nose. I've lost faith in him since. Oh - it's Hooligan, is it? I'm glad of that; Hooligan's a dear - and he has the easiest gallop of any horse on the ranch. Have you tried him yet, Ford?"

The heart of Ford lifted in his chest at her tone and her words, along toward the last. He forgot the chill of her voice in the beginning, and he dwelt greedily upon the fact that once more she had called him Ford. But his joy died suddenly when he led his horse out and discovered that Dick and Jim Felton were coming down the path, within easy hearing of her. Ford did not know women very well, but most men are born with a rudimentary understanding of them. He suspected that her intimacy of tone was meant for Dick's benefit; and when they had ridden three or four miles and her share of the conversation during that time had consisted of "yes" twice, "no" three times, and one "indeed," he was sure of it.

So Ford began to wonder why she came at all - unless that, also, was meant to discipline Dick - and his own mood became a silent one. He did not, he told himself indignantly, much relish being used as a club to beat some other man into good behavior.

They rode almost to Long Ridge before Ford discovered that Josephine was stealing glances at his face whenever she thought he was not looking, and that the glances were questioning, and might almost be called timid. He waited until he was sure he was not mistaken, and then turned his head unexpectedly, and smiled into her startled eyes.

"What is it?" he asked, still smiling at her. "I won't bite. Say it, why don't you?"

She bit her lips and looked away.

"I wanted to ask something - ask you to do something," she said, after a minute. And then hurriedly, as if she

B. M. Bower

feared her courage might ebb and leave her stranded, "I wish you'd give me that - jug!"

Sheer surprise held Ford silent, staring at her.

"I don't ask many favors - I wish you'd grant just that one. I wouldn't ask another."

"What do you want of it?"

"Oh -" she stopped, then plunged on recklessly. "It's getting on my nerves so! And if you gave it to me, you wouldn't have to fight the temptation -"

"Why wouldn't I? There's plenty more where that came from," he reminded her.

"But it wouldn't be right where you could get it any time the craving came. Won't you let me take it?" He had never before heard that tone from her; but he fought down the thrill of it and held himself rigidly calm.

"Oh, I don't know - the jug's doing all right, where it is," he evaded; what he wanted most was to get at her real object, and, man-like, to know beyond doubt whether she really cared.

"But you don't - you never touch it," she urged. "I know, because - well, because every day I look into it! I suppose you'll say I have no right, that it's spying, or something. But I don't care for that. And I can see that it's worrying you dreadfully. And if you don't drink any of it, why won't you let me have it?"

"If I don't drink it; what difference does it make who

has it?" he countered.

"I'm afraid there'll be a time when you'll yield, just because you are blue and discouraged - or something; whatever mood it is that makes the temptation hardest to resist. I know myself that things are harder to endure some days than they are others." She stopped and looked at him in that enigmatical way she had. "You may not know it - but I've been staying here just to see whether you fail or succeed. I thought I understood a little of why you came, and I - I stayed." She leaned and twisted a wisp of Hooligan's mane nervously, and Ford noticed how the color came and went in the cheek nearest him.

"I - oh, it's awfully hard to say what I want to say, and not have it sound different," she began again, without looking at him. "But if you don't understand what I mean -" Her teeth clicked suggestively.

Ford leaned to her. "Say it anyway and take a chance," he urged, and his voice was like a kiss, whether he knew it or not. He did know that she caught her breath at the words or the tone, and that the color flamed a deeper tint in her cheek and then faded to a faint glow.

"What I mean is that I appreciate the way you have acted all along. I - it wasn't an easy situation to meet, and you have met it like a man - and a gentleman. I was afraid of you at first, and I misunderstood you completely. I'm ashamed to confess it, but it's true. And I want to see you make good in this thing you have attempted; and if there's anything on earth that I can do to help you, I want you to let me do it. You will, won't you?" She looked at him then with clear, honest eyes. "It's my way of wanting to thank you for -

B. M. Bower

for not taking any advantage, or trying to, of - your - position that night."

Ford's own cheeks went hot. "I thought you knew all along that I wasn't a cur, at least," he said harshly. "I never knew before that you had any reason to be afraid of me, that night. If I'd known that - but I thought you just didn't like me, and let it go at that. And what I said I meant. You needn't feel that you have anything to thank me for; I haven't done a thing that deserves thanks - or fear either, for that matter."

"I thought you understood, when I left -"

"I didn't worry much about it, one way or the other," he cut in. "I hunted around for you, of course, and when I saw you'd pulled out for good, I went over the hill and camped. I didn't get the note till next morning; and I don't know," he added, with a brief smile, "as that did much toward making me understand. You just said to wait till some one came after me. Well, I didn't wait." He laughed and leaned toward her again. "Now there seems a chance of our being - pretty good friends," he said, in the caressing tone he had used before, and of which he was utterly unconscious, "we won't quarrel about that night, will we? You got home all right, and so did I. We'll forget all about it. Won't we?" He laid a hand on the horn of her saddle so that they rode close together, and tried futilely to read what was in her face, since she did not speak.

Josephine stared blankly at the brown slope before them. Her lips were set firmly together, and her brows were contracted also, and her gloved fingers gripped the reins tightly. She paid not the slightest attention to Ford's hand upon her saddle horn, nor at the steady gaze of his eyes. Later, when Ford observed the rigidity of her whole pose and sensed that mental withdrawing which needs no speech to push one off from the more intimate ground of companionship, he wondered a little. Without in the least knowing why he felt rebuffed, he took away his hand, and swung his horse slightly away from her; his own back stiffened a little in response to the chilled atmosphere.

"Yes," she said at last, "we'll forget all about it, Mr. Campbell."

"You called me Ford, a while ago," he hinted.

"Did I? One forms the habit of picking up a man's given name, out here in the West, I find. I'm sorry -"

"I don't want you to be sorry. I want you to do it again. All the time," he added boldly.

He caught the gleam of her eyes under her heavy lashes, as she glanced at him sidelong.

"If you go looking at me out of the corner of your eyes," he threatened recklessly, kicking his horse closer, "I'm liable to kiss you!"

And he did, before she could draw away.

"I've been kinda thinking maybe I'm in love with you, Josephine," he murmured, holding her close. "And now I'm dead sure of it. And if you won't love me back why - there'll be something doing, that's all!"

"Yes? And what would you do, please?" Her tone was icy, but he somehow felt that the ice was very, very thin, and that her heart beat warm beneath. She drew herself free, and he let her go.

"I dunno," he confessed whimsically. "But Lordy me! I'd sure do something!"

"Look for comfort in that jug, I suppose you mean?"

"No, I don't mean that." He stopped and considered, his forehead creased as if he were half angry at the imputation. "I'm pretty sure of where I stand, on that subject. I've done a lot of thinking, since I hit the Double Cross - and I've cut out whisky for good.

"I know what you thought, and what Mrs. Kate thinks yet; and I'll admit it was mighty tough scratching for a couple of days after I got hold of that jug. But I found out which was master - and it wasn't the booze!" He looked at her with eyes that shone. "Josie, girl, I took a long chance - but I put it up to myself this way, when the jug seemed to be on top. I told myself it was whisky or you; not that exactly, either. It's hard to say just what I do mean. Not you, maybe - but what you stand for. What I could get out of life, if I was straight and lived clean, and had a little woman like you. It may not be you at all; that's as you -"

He stopped as if some one had laid a hand over his mouth. It was not as she said. It might have been, only for that drunken marriage of his. Never before had he hated whisky as bitterly as he did then, when he remembered what it had done for him that night in Sunset, and what it was doing now. It closed his lips upon what he would have given much to be able to say; for he was a man with all the instincts of chivalry and honor - and he loved the girl. It was, he realized bitterly, just because he did love her so well, that he could not say more. He had said too much already; but her nearness had gone to his head, and he had forgotten that he was not free to say what he felt.

Perhaps Josephine mistook his sudden silence for trepidation, or humility. At any rate she reined impulsively close, and reached out and caught the hand hanging idly at his side.

"Ford, I'm no coquette," she said straightforwardly, with a blush for maiden-modesty's sake. "I believe you; absolutely and utterly I believe you. If you had been different at first - if you had made any overtures whatever toward - toward lovemaking, I should have despised you. I never would have loved you in this world! But you didn't. You kept at such a distance that I - I couldn't help thinking about you and studying you. And lately - when I knew you were fighting the - the habit - I loved you for the way you did fight. I was afraid, too. I used to slip into your room every time you left it, and look - and I just ached to help you! But I knew I couldn't do a thing; and that was the hardest part. All I could do was stand back - clear back out of sight, and hope. And - and love you, too, Ford. I'm proud of you! I'm proud to think that I - I love a man that is a man; that doesn't sit down and whine because a fight is hard, or give up and say it's no use. I do despise a moral weakling, Ford. I don't mind what you have been; it's what you are, that counts with me. And you're a man, every inch of you. I'm not a bit afraid you'll weaken. Only," she added half apologetically, "I did want you to give me the - the jug, because I couldn't bear to see you look so worried." She gave his fingers an adorable little squeeze, and flung his hand away from her, and laughed in a way to set his heart pounding heavily in his chest. "Now you know where I stand, Mr. Man," she cried lightly, "so let's say no more about it. I bet I can beat you across this flat!" She laughed again, wrinkled her nose at him impertinently, and was off in a run.

If she had waited, Ford would have told her. If she had given him a chance, he would have told her afterward; but she did not. She was extremely careful not to let their talk become intimate, after that. She laughed, she raced Hooligan almost to the point of abuse, she chattered about everything under the sun that came into her mind, except their own personal affairs or anything that could possibly lead up to the subject.

Ford, for a time, watched for an opening honestly; saw at last the impossibility of telling her - unless indeed he shouted, "Say, I'm a married man!" to her without preface or extenuating explanation - and yielded finally to the reprieve the fates sent him.

CHAPTER XVI

TO FIND AND FREE A WIFE

Ford spent the rest of that day and all of the night that followed, in thinking what would be the best and the easiest method of gaining the point he wished to reach. All along he had been uncomfortably aware of his matrimonial entanglement and had meant, as soon as he conveniently could, to try and discover who was his wife, and how best to free himself and her. He had half expected that she herself would do something to clear the mystery. She had precipitated the marriage, he constantly reminded himself, and it was reasonable to expect that she would do something; though what, Ford could only conjecture.

When he faced Josephine across the breakfast table the next morning, and caught the shy glance she gave him when Mrs. Kate was not looking, a plan he had half formed crystallized into a determination. He would not tell her anything about it until he knew just what he was up against, and how long it was going to take him to free himself. And since he could not do anything about it while he rode and planned and gave orders at the Double Cross, he swallowed his breakfast rather hurriedly and went out to find Jim Felton.

"Say, Jim," he began, when he ran that individual to

earth in the stable, where, with a pair of sheep shears, he was roaching the mane of a shaggy old cow pony to please Buddy, who wanted to make him look like a circus horse, even if there was no hope of his ever acting like one. "I'm going to hand you the lines and let you drive, for a few days. I've got to scout around on business of my own, and I don't know just how long it's going to take me. I'm going right away - to-day."

"Yeah?" Jim poised the shears in air and regarded him quizzically over the pony's neck. "Going to pass me foreman's privilege - to hire and fire?" he grinned. "Because I may as well tell you that if you do, Dick won't be far behind you on the trail."

"Oh, darn Dick. I'll fire him myself, maybe, before I leave. Yes," he added, thinking swiftly of Josephine as the object of Dick's desires, "that's what I'll do. Maybe it'll save a lot of trouble while I'm gone. He's a tricky son-of-a-gun."

"You're dead right; he is," Jim agreed. And then, dryly: "Grandmother just died?"

"Oh, shut up. This ain't an excuse - it's business. I've just got to go, and that's all there is to it. I'll fix things with the missus, and tell her you're in charge. Anyway, I won't be gone any longer than I can help."

"I believe that, too," said Jim softly, and busied himself with the shears.

Ford looked at him sharply, in doubt as to just how much or how little Jim meant by that. He finally shrugged his shoulders and went away to tell Mrs. Kate, and found that a matter which required more diplomacy than he ever suspected he possessed. But he did tell her, and he hoped that she believed the reason he gave for going, and also had some faith in his assurance that he would be back, probably, in a couple of days - or as soon afterwards as might be.

"There's nothing but chores to do now around the ranch, and Jack will ride fence," he explained unnecessarily, to cover his discomfort at her coldness. "Jim can look after things just as well as I can. There won't be any need to start feeding the calves, unless it storms; and if it does, Jim and Jack will go ahead, all right. I'm going to let Dick and Curly go. We don't need more than two men besides Walt, from now on."

"I wish Chester was here," said Mrs. Kate ambiguously.

Ford did not ask her why she wished that. He told her good-by as hastily as if he had to run to catch a train, and left her. He hoped he would be lucky enough to see Josephine - and then he hoped quite as sincerely that he would not see her, after all. It would be easier to go without her clear eyes asking him why.

What he meant to do first was to find Rock, and see if he had been sober enough that night in Sunset to remember what happened at the marriage ceremony, and could give him some clue as to the woman's identity and whereabouts. If he failed there, he intended to hunt up the preacher. That, also, presented certain difficulties, but Ford was in the mood to overcome obstacles. Once he discovered who the woman was, it seemed to him that there should be no great amount of trouble in getting free. As he understood it, he was not the man she had intended to

B. M. Bower

marry; and not being the man she wanted, she certainly could not be over-anxious to cling to him.

While he galloped down the trail to town, he went over the whole thing again in his mind, to see if there might be some simpler plan than the one he had formed in the night.

"No, sir - it's Rock I've got to see first," he concluded. "But Lord only knows where I'll find him; Rock never does camp twice in the same place. Never knew him to stay more than a month with one outfit. But I'll find him, all right!"

And by one of those odd twists of circumstances which sets men to wondering if there is such a thing as telepathy and a specifically guiding hand and the like, it was Rock and none other whom he met fairly in the trail before he had gone another mile.

"Well, I'll be gol darned!" Ford whispered incredulously to himself, and pulled up short in the trail to wait for him.

Rock came loping up with elbows flapping loosely, as was his ungainly habit. His grin was wide and golden as of yore, his hat at the same angle over his right eyebrow.

"Gawd bless you, brother! May peace ride behind your cantle!" he declaimed unctuously, for Rock was a character, in his way, and in his speech was not in the least like other men. "Whither wendest thou?"

"My wending is all over for the present," said Ford, wheeling his horse short around, that he might ride alongside the other. "I started out to hunt you up, you old devil. How are you, anyway?"

"It is well with me, and well with my soul - what little I've got - but it ain't so well with my winter grub-stake. I'm just as tickled to see you as you ever dare be to meet up with me, and that's no lie. I heard you've got a stand-in with the Double Cross, and seeing they ain't on to my little peculiarities, I thought I'd ride out and see if I couldn't work you for a soft snap. Got any ducks out there you want led to water?"

"Maybe - I dunno. I just canned two men this morning, before I left." Ford was debating with himself how best to approach the subject to him most important.

"Good ee-nough! I can take the place of those two men; eat their share of grub, do their share of snoring, and shirk their share of work, and drink their share of booze - oh, lovely! But, in the words of the dead, immortal Shakespeare, 'What's eating you?' You look to me as if you hadn't enjoyed the delights of a good, stiff jag since -" He waved a hand vaguely. "Ain't a scar on you, so help me!" He regarded Ford with frank curiosity.

"Oh, yes there is. I've got the hide peeled off two knuckles, and one of my thumbs is just getting so it will move without being greased," Ford assured him, and then went straight at what was on his mind.

"Say, Rock, I was told that you had a hand in my getting married, back in Sunset that night."

Rock made his horse back until it nearly fell over a rock; his face showed exaggerated symptoms of terror.

B. M. Bower

"I couldn't help it," he wailed. "Spare muh - for muh poor mother's sake, oh spare muh life!" Whereat Ford laughed, just as Rock meant that he should do. "You licked Bill twice for that, they tell me," Rock went on, quitting his foolery and coming up close again. "And you licked the preacher that night, and - so the tale runneth - like to have put the whole town on the jinks. Is there anything in particular you'd like to do to me?"

"I just want you to tell me who I married - if you can." Ford reddened as the other stared, but he did not stop. "I was so darned full that night I let the whole business ooze out of my memory, and I haven't been able to -"

Rock was leaning over the saddle horn, howling and watery-eyed. Ford looked at him with a dawning suspicion.

"It did strike me, once or twice," he said grimly, "that the whole thing was a put-up job. If you fellows rigged up a josh like that, and let it go as far as this, may the Lord have mercy on your souls, for I won't!"

But Rock could only wave him off weakly; so Ford waited until he had recovered. Even then, it took some talking to convince Rock that the affair was truly serious and not to be treated any longer as a joke.

"Why, damn it, man, I'm in love with a girl and I want to marry her if I can get rid of this other darned, mysterious, Tom-fool of a woman," Ford gritted at last, in sheer desperation. "Or if it's just a josh, by this and by that I mean to find it out."

Rock sobered then. "It ain't any josh," he said, with convincing earnestness. "You got married, all right enough. And if it's as you say, Ford, I sure am sorry for it. I don't know the girl's name. I'd know her quick enough if I should see her, but I can't tell you who she was."

Ford swore, of course. And Rock listened sympathetically until he was done.

"That's the stuff; get it out of your system, Ford, and then you'll feel better. Then we can put our heads together and see if there isn't some way to beat this combination."

"Could you spot the preacher, do you reckon?" asked Ford more calmly.

"I could - if he didn't see us coming," Rock admitted guardedly. "Name of Sanderson, I believe. I've seen him around Garbin. He could tell - he must have some record of it; but would he?"

"Don't you know, even, why she came and glommed onto me like that?" Ford's face was as anxious as his tone.

"Only what you told me, confidentially, in a corner afterwards," said Rock regretfully. "Maybe you told it straight, and maybe you didn't; there's no banking on a man's imagination when he's soused. But the way you told it to me was this:

"You said the girl told you that she was working for some queer old party - an old lady with lots of dough; and she made her will and give her money all to some institution - hospital or some darned thing, I forget just what, or else you didn't say. Only, if this girl would marry her son within a certain time, he could have the wad. Seems the son was something of a high-roller, and the old lady knew he'd blow it in, if it was turned over to him without any ballast, like; and the girl was supposed to be the ballast, to hold him steady. So the old lady, or else it was the girl, writes to this fellow, and he agrees to hook up with the lady and take the money and behave himself. Near as I could make it out, the time was just about up before the girl took matters into her own hand, and come out on a hunt for this Frank Cameron. How she happened to sink her rope on you instead, and take her turns before she found out her mistake, you'll have to ask her - if you ever see her again.

"But this much you told me - and I think you got it straight. The girl was willing to marry you - or Frank Cameron - so he could get what belonged to him. She wasn't going to do any more, though, and you told me" - Rock's manner became very impressive here - "that you promised her, as a man and a gentleman, that you wouldn't ever bother her, and that she was to travel her own trail, and she didn't want the money. She just wanted to dodge that fool will, seems like. Strikes me I'd a let the fellow go plumb to Guinea, if I was in her place, but women get queer notions of duty, and the like of that, sometimes. Looks to me like a fool thing for a woman to do, anyway."

Though they talked a good while about it, that was all the real information which Ford could gain. He would have to find the minister and persuade him to show the record of the marriage, and after that he would have to find the girl.

Before they reached that definite conclusion, the storm

which had been brewing for several days swooped down upon them, and drove Ford to the alternative of riding in the teeth of it to town, which was not only unpleasant but dangerous, if it grew any worse, or retracing his steps to the Double Cross and waiting there until it was over. So that is what he did, with Rock to bear him willing company.

They met Dick and Curly on the way, and though Ford stopped them and suggested that they turn back also, neither would do so. Curly intimated plainly that the joys of town were calling to him from afar, and that facing a storm was merely calculated to make his destination more alluring by contrast. "Turn back with two months' wages burning up my inside pocket? Oh, no!" he laughed, and rode on. Dick did not say why, but he rode on also. Ford turned in the saddle and looked after them, as they disappeared in a swirl of fine snow.

"That's what I ought to do," he said, "but I'm not going to do it, all the same."

"Which only goes to prove," bantered Rock, "that the Double Cross pulls harder than all the preacher could tell you. I wonder if there isn't a girl at the Double Cross, now!"

"There is," Ford confessed, with a grin of embarrassment. "And you shut up."

"I just had a hunch there was," Rock permitted himself to say meekly, before he dropped the subject.

It was ten minutes before Ford spoke again.

"I'll take you up to the house and introduce you to her, Rock, if you'll behave yourself," he offered then, with a shyness in his manner that nearly set Rock off in one of his convulsions of mirth. "But the missus isn't wise - so watch out. And if you don't behave yourself," he added darkly, "I'll knock your block off."

"Sure. But my block is going to remain right where it's at," Rock assured him, which was a tacit promise of as perfect behavior as he could attain.

They looked like snow men when they unsaddled, with the powdery snow beaten into the very fabric of their clothing, and Ford suggested that they go first to the bunk-house to thaw out. "I'd sure hate to pack all this snow into Mrs. Kate's parlor," he added whimsically. "She's the kind of housekeeper that grabs the broom the minute you're gone, to sweep your tracks off the carpet. Awful nice little woman, but -"

"But not The One," chuckled Rock, treading close upon Ford's heels. "And I'll bet fifteen cents," he offered rashly, looking up, "that the person hitting the high places for the bunk-house is The One."

"How do you know?" Ford demanded, while his eyes gladdened at sight of Josephine, with a Navajo blanket flung over her head, running down the path through the blizzard to the bunk-house kitchen.

"'Cause she shied when she saw you coming. Came pretty near breaking back on you, too," Rock explained shrewdly.

They reached the kitchen together, and Ford threw open the door, and held it for her to pass.

"I came after some of Mose's mince-meat," she explained hastily. "It's a terrible storm, isn't it? I'm glad it didn't strike yesterday. I thought you were going to be gone for several days."

Ford, with embarrassed haste to match her own, presented Rock in the same breath with wishing that Rock was elsewhere; for Mose was not in the kitchen, and he had not had more than a few words with her for twenty-four hours. He was perilously close to forgetting his legal halter when he looked at her.

She was, he thought, about as sweet a picture of a woman as a man need ever look upon, as she stood there with the red Navajo blanket falling back from her dark hair, and with her wide, honest eyes fixed upon Rock. She was blushing, as if she, too, wished Rock elsewhere. She turned impulsively, set down the basin she had been holding in her arm, and pulled the blanket up so that it framed her face bewitchingly.

"Mose can bring up the mince-meat when he comes - since he isn't here," she said hurriedly. "We weren't looking for you back, but dinner will be ready in half an hour or so, I think." She pulled open the door and went out into the storm.

Rock stared at the door, still quivering with the slam she had given it. Then he looked at Ford, and afterward sat down weakly upon a stool, and began dazedly pulling the icicles from his mustache.

"Well - I'll - be - cremated!" he said in a whisper.

"And what's eating you, Rock?" Ford quizzed gayly. He had seen something in the eyes of Josephine, when he met her, that had set his blood jumping again. "Did Miss Melby -"

"Miss Melby my granny!" grunted Rock, in deep disgust. "That there is your wife!"

Ford backed up against the wall and stared at him blankly. Afterward he took a deep breath and went out as though the place was on fire.

CHAPTER XVII

WHAT FORD FOUND AT THE TOP

Ford Campbell was essentially a man of action; he did not waste ten seconds in trying to deduce the whys and hows of the amazing fact; he would have a whole lifetime in which to study them. He started for the house, and the tracks he made in the loose, shifting snow were considerably more than a yard apart. He even forgot to stamp off the clinging snow and scour his boot-soles upon the porch rug, and when he went striding in, he pushed the door only half shut behind him, so that it swung in the wind and let a small drift collect upon the parlor carpet, until Mrs. Kate, feeling a draught, discovered it, and was shocked beyond words at the sacrilege.

Ford went into the dining-room, crossed it in just three strides, and ran his quarry to earth in the kitchen, where she was distraitly setting out biscuit materials. He started toward her, realized suddenly that the all-observing Buddy was at his very heels, and delayed the reckoning while he led that terrible man-child to his mother.

"I wish you'd close-herd this kid for about four hours," he told Mrs. Kate bluntly, and left her looking scared and unconsciously posing as protective motherhood, her arm around the outraged Robert Chester Mason. Mrs. Kate was absolutely convinced that Ford was at last really drunk and "on the rampage," and she had a terrible vision of slain girlhood in the kitchen, so that she was torn between mother-love and her desire to protect Phenie. But Ford had looked so threateningly at her and Buddy that she could not bring herself to attract his attention to the child or herself. Phenie had plenty of spirit; she could run down to the bunk-house - Mrs. Kate heard a door slam then, and shuddered. Phenie, she judged swiftly, had locked herself into the pantry.

Phenie had. Or, to be exact, she had run in and slammed the door shut in Ford's very face, and she was leaning her weight against it. Mrs. Kate, pressing the struggling Buddy closer to her, heard voices, a slight commotion, and then silence. She could bear no more. She threw a shawl over her head, grasped Buddy firmly by the arm, and fled in terror to the bunk-house.

The voices were a brief altercation between Ford and Josephine, on the subject of opening the door, before it was removed violently from its hinges. The commotion was when Josephine, between tears and laughter, failed to hold the door against the pressure of a strong man upon the other side, and, suddenly giving over the attempt, was launched against a shelf and dislodged three tin pans, which she barely saved from falling with a great clatter to the floor. The silence - the silence should explain itself; but since humanity is afflicted with curiosity, and demands details, this is what occurred immediately after Josephine had been kissed four times for her stubbornness, and the pans had been restored to their proper place.

"Say! Are you my wife?" was the abrupt question which Ford asked, and kissed her again while he waited for an answer.

"Why, yes - what makes you ask that? Of course I am; that is -" Josephine twisted in his arms, so that she could look into his face. She did not laugh at him, however. She was staring at him with that keen, measuring look which had so incensed him, when he had first met her. "I don't understand you at all, Ford," she said at last, with a frown of puzzlement. "I never have, for that matter. I'd think I was beginning to, and then you would say or do something that would put me all at sea. What do you mean, anyway?"

Ford told her what he meant; told her humbly, truthfully, with never an excuse for himself. And it speaks well for the good sense of Josephine that she heard him through with neither tears, laughter, nor anger to mar his trust in her.

"Of course, I knew you had been drinking, that night," she said, when his story was done, and his face was pressed lightly against the white parting in her soft, brown hair. "I saw it, after - after the ceremony. You - you were going to kiss me, and I caught the odor of liquor, and I felt that you wouldn't have done that if you had been yourself; it frightened me, a little. But you talked perfectly straight, and I never knew you weren't the man - Frank Cameron - until you came here. Then I saw you couldn't be he. Chester had known you when Frank was at home with his mother - I compared dates and was sure of that - and he called you Ford Campbell. So then I saw what a horrible blunder I'd made, and I was worried nearly to death! But I couldn't see what I could do about it, and you didn't -"

"Say, what about this Frank Cameron, anyway?" Ford demanded, with true male jealousy. "What did you want to marry him for? You couldn't have known him, or -"

"Oh, you wouldn't understand -" Josephine gave a little, impatient turn of the head, "unless you knew his mother. I did know Frank, a long time ago, when I was twelve or thirteen, and when I saw you, I thought he'd changed a lot. But it was his mother; she was the dearest thing, but - queer. Sort of childish, you know. And she just worshiped Frank, and used to watch for the postman - oh, it was too pitiful! Sometimes I'd write a letter myself, and pretend it was from him, and read it to her; her eyes were bad, so it was easy -"

"Where was this Frank?" Ford interrupted.

"Oh, I don't know! I never did know. Somewhere out West, we thought. I used to make believe the letters came from Helena, or Butte, because that was where she heard from him last. He was always promising to come home - in the letters. That used to make her so much better," she explained naively. "And sometimes she'd be able to go out in the yard and fuss with her flowers, after one like that. But he never came, and so she got the notion that he was wild and a spendthrift. I suppose he was, or he'd have written, or something. She had lots and lots of money and property, you know.

"Well," Josephine took one of Ford's hand and patted it reassuringly, "she got the notion that I must marry Frank, when he came home. I tried to reason her out of that, and it only made her worse. It grew on her, and I got so I couldn't bear to write any more letters, and that made it worse still. She made a will that I must marry Frank within a year after she died, or he wouldn't get anything but a hundred dollars - and she was worth thousands and thousands." Josephine snuggled closer. "She was shrewd, too. I was not to get anything except a few trinkets. And if we didn't marry, the money would all go to an old ladies' home.

"So, when she died, I felt as if I ought to do something, you see. It didn't seem right to let him lose the property, even if he wouldn't write to his mother. So I had the lawyers try to find him. I thought I could marry him, and let him get the property, and then - well, I counted on getting a divorce." She looked up quickly into Ford's face.

"And you know you did promise not to bother me - just to desert me, you see, so I could get a divorce in a year. I thought I'd come and live with Kate till the year was up, and then get a divorce, and go back home to work. My father left me enough to squeak along on, you see, if I lived in the country. Aunt Ida - that's Frank's mother - paid me a salary for staying with her and looking after her house and her rents and things. And then, when you followed me out here, I was furious! Just simply furious!" She bent her head and set her teeth gently into the fleshy part of Ford's thumb, and Ford flinched. It happened to be the sore one.

"Well, but that doesn't explain how you got your loop on me, girlie - though I sure am glad that you did!"

"Why, don't you see, the time was almost up, just for

all the world like a play. 'Only one day more - and I must save the pa-apers!' So the lawyer Aunt Ida had for years, heard that Frank was - or had been - at Garbin. I rushed out here, and heard that there was a Cameron (only they must have meant Campbell) at Sunset. So I got a license, and the Reverend Sanderson, and took the evening train down there. At the hotel I asked for Mr. Cameron, and they sent you in. And you know the rest, you - you old fraud! How you palmed yourself off on me -"

"I never did! I must have just been in one of my obliging moods; and a man would have to be mighty rude and unkind not to say yes to a pretty girl when -"

That is as far as the discussion went, with anything like continuity or coherence even. Later, however, Josephine did protest somewhat muffledly: "But, Ford, I married you under the name of Frank Cameron, so I don't believe - and anyway - I'd like a real wedding - and a ring!"

Mrs. Kate, having been solemnly assured by Rock that Ford was sober and as nearly in his right mind as a man violently in love can be (Rock made it plain, by implication at least, that he did not consider that very near), ventured into the kitchen just then. She still looked scared and uncertain, until, through the half-open door of the pantry, she heard soft, whispery sounds like kissing - when the kissing is a rapture rather than a ceremony. Mrs. Kate had only been married eight years or so, and she had a good memory. She backed from the kitchen on her toes, and pulled the door shut with the caution of a thief. She did more; she permitted dinner to be an hour late, rather than disturb those two in the pantry.

*   *   *   *   *

The uphill climb was no climb at all, after that. For when a man has found the one woman in the world, and with her that elusive thing we call happiness, even the demon must perforce sheathe his claws and retire, discomfited, to the pit whence he came.

There was a period of impatient waiting, because Josephine and Mrs. Kate both stoutly maintained that the "real wedding" could not take place until Chester came back. After that, there was a Mrs. foreman at the Double Cross until spring. And after that, there was a new ranch and a new house and a new home where happiness came and dwelt unhindered.

B. M. Bower

Choose from Thousands of 1stWorldLibrary Classics By

A. M. Barnard
Ada Leverson
Adolphus William Ward
Aesop
Agatha Christie
Alexander Aaronsohn
Alexander Kielland
Alexandre Dumas
Alfred Gatty
Alfred Ollivant
Alice Duer Miller
Alice Turner Curtis
Alice Dunbar
Ambrose Bierce
Amelia E. Barr
Amory H. Bradford
Andrew Lang
Andrew McFarland Davis
Andy Adams
Anna Sewell
Annie Besant
Annie Hamilton Donnell
Annie Payson Call
Annonaymous
Anton Chekhov
Arnold Bennett
Arthur Conan Doyle
Arthur M. Winfield
Arthur Ransome
Atticus
B.H. Baden-Powell
B. M. Bower
Baroness Emmuska Orczy
Baroness Orczy
Basil King
Bayard Taylor
Ben Macomber
Bertha Muzzy Bower
Bjornstjerne Bjornson
Booth Tarkington
Boyd Cable
Bram Stoker
C. Collodi
C. E. Orr
C. M. Ingleby
Carolyn Wells
Catherine Parr Traill
Charles A. Eastman
Charles Dickens

Charles Dudley Warner
Charles Farrar Browne
Charles Ives
Charles Kingsley
Charles Klein
Charles Amory Beach
Charles Hanson Towne
Charles Lathrop Pack
Charles Whibley
Charles Willing Beale
Charlotte M. Braeme
Charlotte M. Yonge
Charlotte Perkins Stetson
Clair W. Hayes
Clarence Day Jr.
Clarence E. Mulford
Clemence Housman
Confucius
Cornelis DeWitt Wilcox
Cyril Burleigh
D. H. Lawrence
Daniel Defoe
David Garnett
Dinah Craik
Don Carlos Janes
Donald Keyhoe
Dorothy Kilner
Dougan Clark
Douglas Fairbanks
E. Nesbit
E.P.Roe
E. Phillips Oppenheim
Earl Barnes
Edgar Rice Burroughs
Edith Van Dyne
Edith Wharton
Edward J. O'Biren
Edward S. Ellis
Edwin L. Arnold
Eleanor Atkins
Eliot Gregory
Elizabeth Gaskell
Elizabeth McCracken
Elizabeth Von Arnim
Ellem Key
Emerson Hough
Emilie F. Carlen
Emily Dickinson
Enid Bagnold

Enilor Macartney Lane
Erasmus W. Jones
Ernie Howard Pie
Ethel Turner
Ethel Watts Mumford
Eugenie Foa
Eugene Wood
Eustace Hale Ball
Evelyn Everett-green
Everard Cotes
F. H. Cheley
F. J. Cross
Federick Austin Ogg
Ferdinand Ossendowski
Francis Bacon
Francis Darwin
Frances Hodgson Burnett
Frances Parkinson Keyes
Frank Gee Patchin
Frank Harris
Frank Jewett Mather
Frank L. Packard
Frank V. Webster
Frederic Stewart Isham
Frederick Trevor Hill
Frederick Winslow Taylor
Friedrich Kerst
Friedrich Nietzsche
Fyodor Dostoyevsky
G.A. Henty
G.K. Chesterton
Gabrielle E. Jackson
Garrett P. Serviss
Gaston Leroux
George A. Warren
George Ade
Geroge Bernard Shaw
George Durston
George Ebers
George Eliot
George Gissing
George MacDonald
George Meredith
George Orwell
George Sylvester Viereck
George Tucker
George W. Cable
George Wharton James
Gertrude Atherton

Grace E. King
Grace Gallatin
Grant Allen
Guillermo A. Sherwell
Gulielma Zollinger
Gustav Flaubert
II. A. Cody
H. B. Irving
H.C. Bailey
H. G. Wells
H. H. Munro
H. Irving Hancock
H. Rider Haggard
H. W. C. Davis
Hamilton Wright Mabie
Hans Christian Andersen
Harold Avery
Harold McGrath
Harriet Beecher Stowe
Harry Houidini
Helent Hunt Jackson
Helen Nicolay
Hendrik Conscience
Hendy David Thoreau
Henri Barbusse
Henrik Ibsen
Henry Adams
Henry Ford
Henry Frost
Henry James
Henry Jones Ford
Henry Seton Merriman
Henry W Longfellow
Herbert A. Giles
Herbert N. Casson
Herman Hesse
Homer
Honore De Balzac
Horace Walpole
Horatio Alger Jr.
Howard Pyle
Howard R. Garis
Hugh Lofting
Hugh Walpole
Humphry Ward
Ian Maclaren
Inez Haynes Gillmore
Irving Bacheller
Israel Abrahams
Ivan Turgenev
J.G.Austin

J. Henri Fabre
J. M. Barrie
J. Macdonald Oxley
J. S. Fletcher
J. S. Knowles
J. Storer Clouston
Jack London
Jacob Abbott
James Allen
James Andrews
James Baldwin
James DeMille
James Joyce
James Lane Allen
James Lane Allen
James Oliver Curwood
James Oppenheim
James Otis
James R. Driscoll
Jane Austen
Janet Aldridge
Jens Peter Jacobsen
Jerome K. Jerome
John Burroughs
John Cournos
John F. Kennedy
John Gay
John Glasworthy
John Habberton
John Joy Bell
John Kendrick Bangs
John Milton
John Philip Sousa
Jonas Lauritz Idemil Lie
Jonathan Swift
Joseph A. Altsheler
Joseph Carey
Joseph Conrad
Joseph E. Badger Jr
Joseph Hergesheimer
Joseph Jacobs
Jules Vernes
Julian Hawthrone
Julie A Lippmann
Justin Huntly McCarthy
Kakuzo Okakura
Kenneth Grahame
Kenneth McGaffey
Kate Langley Bosher
Kate Langley Bosher
Katherine Cecil Thurston

Katherine Stokes
L. A. Abbot
L. T. Meade
L. Frank Baum
Latta Griswold
Laura Lee Hope
Laurence Housman
Lawrence Beasley
Leo Tolstoy
Leonid Andreyev
Lewis Carroll
Lewis Sperry Chafer
Lilian Bell
Lloyd Osbourne
Louis Hughes
Louis Tracy
Louisa May Alcott
Lucy Fitch Perkins
Lucy Maud Montgomery
Lydia Miller Middleton
Lyndon Orr
M. Corvus
M. H. Adams
Margaret E. Sangster
Margaret Vandercook
Margret Penrose
Maria Edgeworth
Maria Thompson Daviess
Mariano Azuela
Marion Polk Angellotti
Mark Overton
Mark Twain
Mary Austin
Mary Catherine Crowley
Mary Cole
Mary Hastings Bradley
Mary Roberts Rinehart
Mary Rowlandson
M. Wollstonecraft Shelley
Maud Lindsay
Max Beerbohm
Myra Kelly
Nathaniel Hawthrone
Nicolo Machiavelli
O. F. Walton
Oscar Wilde
Owen Johnson
P.G. Wodehouse
Paul and Mabel Thorne
Paul G. Tomlinson
Paul Severing

Percy Brebner
Peter B. Kyne
Plato
R. Derby Holmes
R. L. Stevenson
R. S. Ball
Rabindranath Tagore
Rahul Alvares
Ralph Bonehill
Ralph Henry Barbour
Ralph Victor
Ralph Waldo Emmerson
Rene Descartes
Rex Beach
Rex E. Beach
Richard Harding Davis
Richard Jefferies
Richard Le Gallienne
Robert Barr
Robert Frost
Robert Gordon Anderson
Robert L. Drake
Robert Lansing
Robert Lynd
Robert Michael Ballantyne
Robert W. Chambers
Rosa Nouchette Carey
Rudyard Kipling
Samuel B. Allison

Samuel Hopkins Adams
Sarah Bernhardt
Sarah C. Hallowell
Selma Lagerlof
Sherwood Anderson
Sigmund Freud
Standish O'Grady
Stanley Weyman
Stella Benson
Stephen Crane
Stewart Edward White
Stijn Streuvels
Swami Abhedananda
Swami Parmananda
T. S. Ackland
T. S. Arthur
The Princess Der Ling
Thomas A. Janvier
Thomas A Kempis
Thomas Anderton
Thomas Bailey Aldrich
Thomas Bulfinch
Thomas De Quincey
Thomas H. Huxley
Thomas Hardy
Thomas More
Thornton W. Burgess
U. S. Grant
Valentine Williams

Various Authors
Vaughan Kester
Victor Appleton
Virginia Woolf
Walter Camp
Walter Scott
Washington Irving
Wilbur Lawton
Wilkie Collins
Willa Cather
Willard F. Baker
William Dean Howells
William le Queux
W. Makepeace Thackeray
William W. Walter
Winston Churchill
Yei Theodora Ozaki
Yogi Ramacharaka
Young E. Allison
Zane Grey